The Same Deep Water

Lisa Swallow

The Same Deep Water

Dedication
For Nick, my travelling companion
And for all those who struggle in the depths

Lisa Swallow

To live is the rarest thing in the world.
Most people exist, that is all. (Oscar Wilde)

Lisa Swallow

CHAPTER ONE

#9 Save someone's life

The rough wooden fence erected to keep people from the edge of the rocky cliff frequently fails. Even if the council erected ten-foot barriers with razor wire, the determined would find their way through. By the time the decision is made to come here, one last obstacle is nothing.

I perch on the fence, the wood digging into my backside as I steady myself and look down. Since I arrived half an hour ago, the sun has sunk lower, the beauty of the sunset over the Indian Ocean lost on my deadened self. Instead, with my long brown hair falling into my face, I focus numbly on the rocks below, knowing my battle is over.

"Careful, you'll fall."

A low voice behind drags me from the moment and I turn my head sharply. I waited near the car park until all the cars left and never expected a newcomer, let alone somebody who'd seek out this place in the dusk. In the fading light, a guy stands nearby, smiling. I barely register him, past the fact he's a young guy with dark blond hair touching his ears, and has a small bunch of white and pink flowers in his hand. Without responding, I turn back to the view to my death.

"I like the view from here, too," he continues.

I grip the fence, splinters pricking my hands and look in surprise as the man sits next to me, ensuring he's at a respectful distance. The growing dusk obscures much of him, but something captures my attention. The man's eyes match the ocean, not cerulean waters on a summer's day, but midnight blue shadowing secrets beneath. His eyes are the colour of the water which stole the girl I once was.

I prop my elbows on my knees and dig my hands into my hair, allowing strands to fall forward and obscure my face from him.

"So, do you come here often?" he asks.

I was prepared to pretend he wasn't here and to wait for him to leave, but his bizarre comment deserves an answer.

"How many people do you think come here more than once?" I ask, twisting my head back to him.

"Not many, I guess. Why are you here?"

"Because I don't want to come here again."

"Want to talk about anything?"

Annoyed he's managed to draw me into conversation, I tip my hair into my face again. The sounds of the waves below call me into the darkness that'd solve everything.

I'm unsure how long I sit and prepare to yield to my brain's whispering plot to kill me, the one that's waited for months and finally succeeded. Almost.

The man doesn't leave, and when I surreptitiously peer out of the side of my hair, he's in the same position, flowers in one hand, tapping his fingers on the fence. His nails are short and neat, hands and arms tanned.

Why am I noticing?

"Did you leave a note?" he asks.

"A note?"

"And sort your affairs out."

"What affairs?"

"Before you jump." He pauses. "I won't stop you

by the way."

His words jolt my heart, the one that I need to stop beating because it keeps alive a person I hate. "Good."

"But I hope you organised everything first."

I shuffle further from him. "What's to organise?"

"Well, who's getting your money? Possessions? I presume you have some since you don't look like you live on the streets."

Possessions. My life is all possessions. Everything I want bought for me, to help me perform my best, to ease the pain. Comfortable and happy and lacking in nothing. An unwanted image of my grandparents trips across my mind and I rub my face, erasing them.

"Or did you just come here without really planning what to do?"

His words are invading my jumbled brain; holding a coherent conversation is something I lost the ability for days ago. "Please be quiet or go away. Or both."

The man shivers slightly against the coastal breeze, fixing me with his sea-blue eyes, drawing me to human contact. "No."

"Why?"

"Because."

"Because what?"

"Do you like flowers?" He holds the bunch out to me and I stare at them. The heads are spoilt by his mishandling and they're still in the cellophane from the store, the price label half-attached.

"No."

"Really? I thought all girls like flowers. Damn." He drops them to the ground. "What do you like?"

"Being on my own," I say pointedly.

"Being is a good start." He stares ahead. "Rather than not being. Isn't there a Shakespeare quote about that somewhere? There's always a Shakespeare quote about love or death."

Death.

"To be or not to be?" I ask.

He laughs. "That's the one. Do you like Shakespeare?"

This man in board shorts and a faded T-shirt isn't somebody I'd pin as a Shakespeare reader, more the kind living an outdoor life far away from books.

"No. Everybody knows that quote," I reply.

"Have you read his work?"

"No."

"Then how can you decide you don't like something you've never seen?" he asks.

"I suppose..."

"Like the future. You don't like the future, but you've never seen it."

"Be quiet. You're making my brain hurt. Move."

The man obeys, shifting away, but remains on the fence, sighing quietly at first then louder until I'm ready to slap him to shut him up.

"What are you doing?" I snap.

"Enjoying the view. You?"

"Waiting for you to go."

"Why?"

"Because you might stop me."

"I said I wouldn't, but I won't leave so you'll have to jump with me here. If you do, please make sure you don't miss and seriously injure yourself because a future as a paraplegic would be more unpleasant than the future you're scared of now."

I swallow down the doubt sneaking in. "I'm not scared of the future."

"No? Then why are you running from it?"

"Shut up."

"You seem like a smart girl, with your Shakespeare quotes and all, I'm sure you can do better than 'shut up' if you don't want to lose an argument."

I glare, clenching my teeth. "Why? Why are you

here?"

"Philosophical or factual question?"

I'm about to tell him to shut up again, but his raised eyebrow prevents me. "You can't sit here with me all night."

"Can't I? I'm a big boy. I can do what I want."

How old is he? Early twenties like I am? Older? He has more bulk than most of the guys my age.

What does any of this matter?

Annoyed at his distraction, I look away again. Stop grounding me; I'm not part of the world.

"I won't try to persuade you what to do, or 'talk you down', don't worry. There's no point telling you to feel guilty about those you'll leave behind, because if you're here, I think you're beyond rational thought about life, or feeling."

"I do feel. I hurt. Everywhere, everything, and I want this to stop!" I blurt. Placing a shaking hand over my mouth, I squeeze my eyes shut, back to the darkness he's reminding me of.

"And you think death stops you hurting?" he asks. "Death doesn't only stop the pain. Death stops everything. Death stops you."

"I know."

"All of you, not just the sick part."

"The sick part is all of me."

"No, it's not. You know that deep down. You can fix this. You can have a new life."

"I thought you weren't going to tell me what to do."

"I'm not. I'm just pointing out the obvious."

Pressure builds in my head, aching as his words assault my dark thoughts. "You're confusing me. Please, again, leave me alone."

He ignores me. "What's your name?"

"What's yours?"

"Guy."

"A guy named Guy," I say with a small laugh.

"Not just any guy."

"I'm sure you're not."

"I'm the guy who's going to save your life." No. I stand and edge forward. I expect him to jump up after me, but he remains still. "And you are...?"

"Done."

"That's an odd name," he replies, deadpan.

I glance over my shoulder. "Do you think you're funny?"

"Not really, suicide girl."

The word slices through my body, into my heart. This is who I'll be. The girl who committed suicide, spoken about, grieved for. But they don't understand how I can't live with this pressure expanding in my skull, the darkness forcing out everything.

"Phe," I snap. "My name is Phe."

"Fi? Fiona?"

"No. Not Fiona."

"Huh. Odd name for an odd girl. Would you like to go for a drink, Phe?" He stands too.

"I don't drink."

His brow furrows for a moment. "Oh. You look old enough."

"I am old enough. I just don't go out much. I prefer my own company."

"That sucks then."

"Why?"

"Jump off there and you'll never have a chance to live life, to take a chance on experiences that leave you more alive than others."

I move closer to the edge, to make a point.

"So many people live lives that are empty and full of nothing, Phe, don't choose emptiness and oblivion when you have so much. You can do so much, believe me."

"You don't know me," I say to the horizon.

"You don't know you. You're too young to know who you are, and your sick brain won't let you learn."

I turn my head. "And how are you so wise? You're not much older than me!"

"Not much wiser either, but take a chance on life."

He keeps doing this. Guy isn't physically pulling me away from the edge, but his words are gradually curling around my body and tugging me back to the world.

"Do you have a bucket list?" he asks.

I look back into his strange eyes, increasingly confused by his random questions. Is this a ploy?

"No."

"You should have one."

"Why? I'm about to die. Do you have one?" I shoot back.

"I do. I haven't got very far with mine though." Guy pulls an A4 sheet of paper out of his pocket, one repeatedly creased through constant folding and unfolding. "I have ten things on the list." Guy runs his finger down his list. "I've done two, eight more to go."

If he's expecting me to ask what the items are, he's wrong.

"Can you be my third? There's something I want to do with you."

Possibilities fly through my mind. He asked me for a drink. Sex with a random girl? Or maybe he's a virgin and wants to cross that off. I appraise his lean body again. Unlikely.

"Something to tick off your list? I'm not that kind of girl."

He laughs and sweeps a gaze over me, his scrutiny irritates me, but Guy's look lingers longer on my eyes than my body. "I'm positive you're not," he says softly. "No, not sex."

Colouring, I look away. The paper rustles and he clears his throat. 'Number Nine: Save someone's life'."

I stare. "You want to save my life so you can tick me off a list?"

"Well, I don't know you, so there's no other reason." He points at the bouquet. "But I did bring flowers."

The forlorn bunch rest on the ground where Guy dropped them, and I kick them. The pink lilies tumble from the edge of the cliff and drop out of site. Guy steps forward and looks over.

"Long way down."

A giddy lurching between my head and stomach, and my body's natural survival instinct kicks in as rock slips from beneath my summer sandals in the direction of the flowers. I stagger back and grab the fence. Guy remains close to the edge and crosses his arms, looking at me.

"So? Can I?" he asks.

"Save my life?"

"Yeah."

"Because of your list?"

"Yep." He pushes his unruly hair from his face. "Plus, you're far too good-looking to be smashed against a load of rocks."

Why do I blush? I inspect my feet, focusing on my painted toenails. I bought the neon pink varnish on a shopping trip with my friend Erica last month. Recently I've worn the colour to pretend I'm a dazzling pink girl, not a girl in a black hole.

"Why not give blood? That would save somebody's life," I retort.

Guy's mouth curls into a smile, accentuating the dimples. "Good-looking and smart, too. That is a very good suggestion. Oh, well, I'm here now. May as well save you."

I dig my nails into my palms, pushing in more pain. Feeling.

"But best make it quick," he says in a casual tone.

"Quick?"

"I don't have long."

"Oh, somewhere you need to be?" I ask sarcastically and glance at him again.

"No, I don't have long to finish my list."

"But it's a bucket list. You have your whole life to finish."

His smile slips. "Like I said, not long."

I grip the fence harder. My world today is cloaked in a surreal fog and Guy's adding to this by the minute. He continues to watch with the same impassive look, becoming harder to see as the sun sets.

"What do you mean you don't have long?" I ask. He nods his head to indicate I should state the obvious. "Do you mean you're... are you sick?"

"Euphemisms. Don't you love them? Dying. I have my bucket list to complete first, though, which is why I don't have time to waste."

I reel as if a sledgehammer just smacked me in the chest, knocking me further from the edge. How can he be so nonchalant, as if telling me he's late for a dinner date?

I'm a selfish, bad person. Here's a dying man who wants to live long enough to fulfill his dreams, and here I am, wanting to die. My thoughts must be evident because Guy steps closer. The shock spreads to my fingers and I squeeze them open and shut, watching them tremble. My fingers feel like part of me again.

"I'm sorry," I whisper.

"Why? You don't know me."

"But you're a good person."

"Am I?"

"You feel like a good person."

"Feel? But you feel nothing, suicide girl."

The lump in my throat chokes back the need to tell him not to call me that. He can't because I'm not.

I won't be. I couldn't with Guy watching me; he has to go. I have to go. I can't do this in front of somebody else.

"Okay." I say. "Save my life."

He straightens. "Seriously?"

"Yes." He can tick me off his list tonight; I can change my mind and come back again.

Guy climbs over the fence, then turns, outstretching a hand. "Let me take you home, Phe."

I tuck my hands beneath my arms and he drops his hand. "Not home."

"Where?"

Sensation seeps back into my limbs, bordering around the edge of my mind but the dreamlike state I've descended into over the last weeks remains. Reality is as tenuous as my change of mind.

"I don't know." I shiver, the evening sea breeze picking at the hairs on my arms.

"Should I call somebody?" he asks.

"I don't know." Erica. No. I can't drag her into this again; she's not responsible and tries to be. Friends should help each other, but the sick friend shouldn't be a burden. Jen doesn't know anything about this side of me. I can't go home.

Guy rubs his face. "How did you get here tonight?"

"Bus. Walked."

"Wait there. Let me fetch something." He turns to leave then pauses before looking back. "You will wait there, won't you?"

Wrapping my arms around myself, I nod. Guy disappears in the direction of the car park. The stars now prick the sky, the waxing moon throwing light on the peace of the place. The fall that beckoned is behind me now. I step further away to the bench across the footpath; the one I sat on as I lost the final fight with myself.

Guy reappears holds a bottle in my direction. "Drink?"

"What is it?"

"Water that pretends to be special because it's flavoured and in a fancy bottle." He holds up a cup. "I have coffee, but it's cold. You can have that instead if you like?"

I take the bottle and grip as he sits next to me. The incessant call of the cicadas and the low sound of cars travelling a nearby road edge into my awareness. Guy gulps his coffee.

"Who were the flowers for?" I ask.

"Whoever wanted them."

He looks ahead, long fingers curled around the cup. "You randomly buy flowers to give to girls?"

"Why not? The flowers are thrown away by the store if they're not sold." He smiles to himself. "I like to see people's reactions."

"I wouldn't expect you find many girls here."

"I stop here on my way home sometimes. I told you, I like the view. I bought the flowers earlier and they were in the car when I saw you." He pauses before adding quietly, "You looked like you really needed some flowers, Phe."

I shiver again. The headache is joined by an exhaustion as I give in to the change in my evening. "That's a strange thing to do."

"So's jumping off rocks."

"True."

The water is cool when I drink, and I hold the water in my mouth, the fizz bubbling against my cheeks as I focus on the flavour. Strawberry? Raspberry? Something more exotic? I swallow. Side by side, we don't look at each other. Is Guy taking glances at me the way I am at him? His fringe reaches his heavy brow and every few minutes he sweeps a strand away, a gesture he probably doesn't realise he's repeating.

Despite the warmth of the evening; my body shakes with the awareness of what I almost did.

"Maybe I should take you to the hospital," he

says.

"No!"

"Okay. But I have to take you somewhere, otherwise, I won't be able to tick you off my list." He flashes me his dimpled smile.

"Your bucket list. Of course."

"Will you write one?"

"Maybe."

"Will you ask somebody for help?"

When I turn my head, he's searching my eyes for the answer he wants. "To write my list?"

"No. To get well. To live your life instead of giving up." The undercurrent of his words is clear in the intensity of the look we share. His is being taken. I'm suddenly overwhelmed by the desire to touch his face, ground myself completely with human contact, and ask him what lies beneath the deep water in his eyes.

"I'll ask for help. Again," I say.

"Good." He stands. "Start with me. Either let me drive you somewhere or call a taxi."

My bag lies in the scrub where I dropped it earlier and I grab the strap.

"Let's go, Phe." As Guy strides away, I hesitate, watching his tall figure as he steps into the shadows. I'm not sure I can trust a man who hangs around suicide spots, with flowers, at dusk.

But why would he save my life if he's going to hurt me?

CHAPTER TWO

Two Months Later

I scrape my hair into a ponytail and snap a band around as I step onto the bus. The bus is cramped with bodies and I squeeze onto half a vacant seat, next to the large woman encroaching on the remaining space. Good thing my backside is smaller than hers. Arms wrapped around her brown leather bag, she doesn't take her eyes of her kindle, and I shuffle to the seat edge, feet dangerously close to tripping anyone else who heads along the aisle.

The journey into the city should be short, but is long thanks to the traffic. I've lived in Perth five months, moved over here from Melbourne after completing my Media degree. I'm not entirely sure how I fought off the competition and won the traineeship as a journalist at *Belle de Jour*, or how long I can hold onto the job without collapsing in a mess – or off a cliff. The fact the popular magazine held the traineeship open for me while I spent time in hospital, then the few weeks after as I took time out, bolsters my confidence. I must've impressed them somehow in the few months before my breakdown, and this vote of confidence adds to my determination to keep moving my life on.

I shudder, casting my mind back to the day I almost became a story in the local news. Sick? Visit medical professionals, they will give you medication and fix you up. Right? Wrong. If there were a magic pill, why would they be making new ones all the time? I fought against what I now know is depression for years as a kid, teen moods darker and deeper than my friends, my reality hidden from everybody but my best friend, Erica. Now she's on the other side of the country. I moved to Perth alone and I share a house with strangers who've become new friends, but I'm alone without Erica.

My working world is full of the beautiful and famous, the airbrushed faces and bodies featured in ads in the magazine beside articles about the latest diets or sexual positions. Lies pull in readers and fool them that they can achieve this reality, that this world exists, and they should emulate the life at all costs. I subscribe to the lie, too, comparing my looks and lifestyle to those around who've succeeded. They act as if happy and free but they are trapped in the fake world they're part of.

Watching the fable constructed around me has the opposite effect than I intended; instead of seeing through the transparency, I use the lies to beat myself up. I'm tall and naturally slender with what my gran constantly calls a 'bonnie face', but all I see are my faults. My less than symmetrical face, the kink in my long, brown hair that prevents me achieving the sleek look without straightening tongs, and I really hate my knees. Yes, my knees. I weigh myself every day, which is ridiculous because my weight hasn't changed for years. The other day I noticed lines forming on my twenty-one year old brow, no surprise really considering the amount of worrying I do. At this rate, I'll have Botox before I'm twenty-five.

Nobody in my current life realises how I obsess. Nobody but Guy has seen past the magazine-print bright and glossy picture I paint of myself. The real Phe is with the memories of death and darkness, safely sealed away again.

To distract myself from the encroaching thoughts, I check work emails on my phone. A message alert sounds and I flick across to the message:

<Have you written your bucket list yet?>

Guy texts me daily; at first it was weekly and then more frequently as time went on. Two months have passed since our weird meeting and we haven't met since, even though we're in the same city. Guy's become a friend, the distant kind you never see, but who's always there to talk to on the outside of real life. Not that we talk about much, and he never talks about himself, mostly he checks in on how I'm going.

Guy's pushing me to start my bucket list, as promised.

The beginning of my list is scrawled on a note pad at home. Guy wants us to meet, compare, and see if there're any we share, that we can do together. I'm wary. The relationship between us can't go beyond this weird connection underlying everything. Guy's part of a night I'd rather forget.

<Haven't you completed all yours yet?> I reply.

<Not even close> How much time does he have? <Compare. Go on. Humour me>

I glance around at the commuters, business-suited and tired even at 8.30 a.m., stuck in their rut. My future life. The bus lurches to a stop and the lady's bag slides off her knee, spilling the contents over the floor. I shove my phone into my bag and bend to help her. She frowns, not meeting my eyes, and grabs the packet of tissues I hand her. No thanks or acknowledgement are offered.

Climbing from the bus, I'm jostled, a guy stands on my toes, and then I'm propelled through the street in the direction of the ten-storey building I work in. On the way, I duck into the coffee shop and wait in line for my morning mocha. Ross, the barista who always has a smile for me is serving, his deep brown eyes sparkle in amusement as I stumble over my words. He has that effect on me. The minute I look into the dark brown eyes that match the chocolate he sprinkles on my morning coffee, I'm lost.

Maybe because of my lack of recent dates, but I fantasise about his full mouth on my lips, and the slender fingers that brush mine when he hands me the cup, stroking my skin. Occasionally, I catch his scent; coffee and vanilla, with a hint of expensive cologne. Once when passing through a department store, I thought I smelled the brand. I doubled back to the men's fragrances section and ran through a selection before the mix of scents confused my brain and the realisation what I was doing embarrassed me.

"For you, lovely Phe," he says with a smile, the words I wish were only for me but are spoken to every girl who passes through here.

"Thanks."

One day I'll say more than my order, my name, and a 'thank you' to Ross, but on the conveyor belt of customers, there's no time to chat. So I return his smile with the false confidence that rests on my surface, and leave.

****

Red pen covers the paper on the desk in front of me, obscuring the majority of the typed text. My body floods with stress, which is processed into head-pounding frustration, then tears threaten. My boss, Pam, could choose a different colour or use pencil. The words scrawled in red mock me, especially the capital 'NO' and 'RE-WRITE'.

Pam began working at *Belle de Jour* in the weeks I was away; my original boss, Nora, was headhunted by a bigger publisher in Sydney and left suddenly. If I'd met

Pam at my initial interview, I doubt I'd have taken the job. Pam knows I'm lucky to have the job, even more so since my absence, and takes advantage of my gratitude. I attempt to keep my head down until I've proven my worth but biting my tongue becomes harder each day.

My daily tasks are everything Pam can't be bothered doing: answering her emails, fielding her phone calls, and fetching lunch from the nearby deli. After large hints from me about learning to write articles, Pam relented and allowed me to, but on something she chose. Excited I might write my first feature piece, my heart sank when I was given a list of facial products to write a comparison of.

This is my fourth draft.

How hard can it be to write an article comparing moisturisers and serums correctly?

I glance around the open plan office, which is half-empty, most people are in meetings I'm not privy to. I should be watching the phones, but the red on the paper steals my patience and I grab my bag. Heading through the expensively furnished room, past the pictures of magazine covers, awards, and accolades, I reach the elevator.

One tear manages to escape my eye and I catch the drop with a finger, cursing. My make-up will run down my face if I don't get a grip.

In the lobby, I pause and pull out my phone.

<Let's compare>

I hit send on the message to Guy.

CHAPTER THREE

The tables outside the small cafe line the pavements, crammed together on a small strip; surrounded by metal chairs that stick to your legs in the height of the Perth summer. There're no menus here, just a chalkboard listing food and drink inside the dark wood panelled building. The places near my workplace are trendy, this one is on the edge of the suburb and popular with locals. After arranging to meet Guy, I composed myself and returned upstairs to work. Several hours later, I wait for him. This is short notice; will he come?

As I sit with my glass of sparkling water, I realise I don't know whereabouts in Perth Guy lives, or how far I've asked him to travel. After half an hour waiting, I shift my chair so I'm beneath the black canvas umbrella and out of the strong sun.

Guy appears and I squint against the bright sunlight as he approaches with a laid-back gait to his walk. A young girl at a nearby table double takes as he passes. Guy stands out amongst the other pedestrians, taller than most with his dark blond hair now touching the edge of his jawline, the muscles on his tanned arms moulded by his blue t-shirt sleeves. I didn't pay full attention the day in the shadows, but this guy – this man – is hot. My mouth dries as he reaches me and as soon as the dark blue eyes meet mine, my heart rate picks up.

I didn't expect this reaction to him.

Guy drags a chair from under my table and sits opposite. "Hey, beautiful girl."

I wrinkle my nose, but his tone suggests this is his a usual greeting for women. "Hello, Guy. How are you?"

Guy pulls a canvas wallet from his shorts pocket. "Such a polite lady. I'm very well, yourself?"

Is he mocking me? "Good, thanks."

His blue eyes capture mine again, crinkling at the edges as he smiles at me. "Liar. What do you want to drink?"

"I'm okay." I indicate the glass of water and he nods.

Weeks of communicating by text have led to a friendship of sorts, but I never expected him to behave as if we're old friends meeting for a quick coffee. Will he mention what happened the last time we met, because this meeting is as if nothing happened?

The condensation runs down the glass and I watch the drops fall as I wait for him to return. Our second face-to-face meeting and his nonchalance matches my nerves. Does he meet a lot of girls? Is that why he's relaxed about the situation?

Guy returns and settles back in his seat with a bottle of Coca-Cola, the old style bottle, then pulls a piece of paper from his board shorts. I smile at the image, my work follows me everywhere because in front of me is a man straight from an ad for summer happiness. Bronzed guys on the beach laughing with bikini-clad girls, eating fast food, and drinking sugar-filled soda. Models with bodies that don't belong to people who eat much at all, and definitely not burgers. All Guy needs to do is lose his t-shirt and he's ticked all the boxes.

"Am I funny?" he asks, unfolding the paper.

"No, you remind me of someone."

"Oh?"

"Just some guy," I say with a half-smile.

He shakes his head. "I knew there was a sense of

humour in there somewhere."

I relax back in my chair, my fear this would be awkward dissipating. Guy's behaviour matches his texts, light-hearted and friendly with no hint of the weirdness that underpins our relationship.

"Thanks for meeting me," I say.

"At last!" He pushes a strand of his fringe away, fixing me with his deep-water eyes. "I was beginning to think you'd bottled on me and I'd never see you again."

"Bottled on you?"

"The bucket list. We're doing some together, remember?" He shakes the paper at me. "I'm looking forward to having some fun with you, Phe."

I look up sharply. A man like him could no doubt persuade any girl with a pulse to have fun with him, but the innuendo isn't matched by any expression that could suggest he's serious.

"You look unhappy. Are you okay?"

"Better than last time we met."

"That's not difficult, is it?" He drinks. "You can't hide behind text messages when we're face to face."

"I'm fine, Guy. Normal everyday stress. Work stuff." I lower my voice. "You know I got help. Things are different. I'm getting better and the dark thoughts have gone."

Guy scrutinises me, and the outside world fades, returning me to the last time he looked inside my soul and yanked me back to reality. Empty of the thoughts controlling my mind that night, others flood in instead.

Who is he?

What's killing him?

Why can't I stop picturing what he looks like under his t-shirt?

Why does he want to know me?

Guy chews on his bottom lip, his own thoughts guarded. "Get it out."

"Pardon?"

"Your list. That's why we're here, isn't it?"

"Oh, right." I pick up my small, black handbag and delve to the bottom. "Sorry."

"That's okay, I'm quite the distraction."

Of course, looking like he does Guy has to be a self-love kind of guy. I give him a small shake of my head and he winks.

My small note pad on the table contrasts with his tattered page ripped at the edges, the large black scrawl much less legible than my neatly printed handwriting.

"We going to read them out?" Guy asks.

My chair is centimetres from touching the one behind and too many people are in earshot of what promises to be a very weird conversation.

"No."

"I'll show you mine, if you show me yours." His mouth twitches with amusement.

"Seriously, Guy?"

"Had to be said." He holds his hand out, palm upwards. "Show me."

As Guy takes my note pad, he pushes his list across the table.

We read, silently, and his list intrigues me:

1. *Swim with sharks.*
2. *Spend a night ghost hunting.*
3. *Visit Hawaii.*
4. *Learn another language.*
5. *Go skydiving.*
6. *See the Van Gogh painting 'Sunflowers'.*
7. *Watch a shooting star.*
8. *Watch the snow fall.*
9. *Save someone's life.*
10. *Fall in love.*

Numbers two and nine are crossed out.

"Not doing them in order then?" I ask.

Guy holds his hand up in a gesture to silence me and to indicate he's still reading, lips pursed. He strokes his chin in an exaggerated pose of a musing professor. "Interesting..."

"What?" This isn't a diary, but the words on the page feel as if they shouldn't be shared.

"One of our items matches. Almost two. 'See a shooting star' is a night together 'sleeping under the stars'." He runs a finger down the list. "These are very girlie: 'swim with dolphins', 'kiss in the rain'."

"Are you judging me? Look at yours! Ghost hunting? At least plan something achievable!"

"Yeah, tried that one at Fremantle Prison. Never found any. Maybe when we go to England, I'll try somewhere else."

"We?"

"The painting I want to see is in England, we're going to England."

"I never said I was doing my list with you!"

"Not all of them, just the ones that match." He rakes his hair from his face as he reads. "Look, I can teach you to surf and help with the tattoo, I know some good artists." Guy lifts the edge of his t-shirt, revealing solid abs decorated with the words *omnia causa fiunt*. I stare, mostly at his muscles to be honest, before he drops the t-shirt.

"Shouldn't we do yours first, if you haven't got... much time," I say.

Guy's face darkens, and he taps his fingers on the table. Maybe I shouldn't have said anything. Guy doesn't look sick, his appearance more alive than people I come across in the 9-5 drudgery. We hardly know each other; whatever illness he has is none of my business. If he wanted to tell me, he would.

"Yeah. True. But I'm two items ahead of you, and you need to catch up. Some we can finish quickly, locally. What do you want to start with?" He studies my list again. "This is an easy one. 'Ask a stranger on a date'. I don't count, by the way."

"This isn't a date! Besides, you asked me weeks ago."

"Yes, but you said no. *You* asked *me* to meet you today."

"This still isn't a date; this is just a meeting between..." I pause. Between what? A girl who almost jumped to her death and the man who stopped her. "Friends."

"Travel buddies."

"If I travel with you."

"We can travel through our lists together," he says and hands back my notebook. "Through your new life and the rest of mine. What do you think?"

I morbidly want to know why and when he'll die. What if he's been given a year and his time runs out because the doctors are wrong?

"So you need to travel soon," I say.

"Soon-ish, but it's the end of January now, and I don't want to visit England in the winter."

"That's the best time to see snow fall."

"Nah, I can see that in Australia, at the snow fields over East. An English summer sounds better. Can you do July?"

"I'm not sure."

"If you can't afford the trip, I'll pay."

The insistence in his demeanour from the night in my darkness returns and I grip onto my assertiveness. "What? No!"

He shrugs. "I'm loaded, may as well spend all my money before I go." I can't help but study his faded t-shirt and the black and blue board shorts. "Yeah, not dressed like I have money, I know." He flicks his black Havaianas against his tanned feet. "I got the designer version of my bogan footwear."

"Very cool."

"I am." Again, the bright grin, but his eyes don't

match.

I drain my glass and wipe the condensation from my hands onto my skirt.

"Another?" he asks.

"No thanks, I have to get back to work."

"Had enough of me already?" He arches a brow. "Two months apart and this is all I get?"

"Sounds like we'll be spending a bit of time together," I say.

"I have all the time in the world for you, Phe." Alarmed at the intensity, at this stunning man eager to spend his remaining time with me, I fight the unusual blushing that flares on my cheeks.

"I'm flattered," I reply.

"So, are you up for this then? Me and you, a step out of life once in a while?"

"What do you mean?"

"I have a list, so do you. I need something in my life to distract me from crap, so do you. How about we get to know each other better, too? Could be fun."

"Really? What kind of fun did you have in mind?"

He grins, revealing the sexy dimples. "Whatever you enjoy doing."

In the bedroom or out? I'm not pursuing that line of thinking. I just met the guy. The real Guy. Sure, Phe, how long do you think you'll hold out against the sexual presence humming around this man?

Guy taps my notepad. "Ten things. I challenge you to one this weekend. Today is Monday, call me later in the week, and tell me which item you've chosen."

"Already?"

"Make it a good one." He drinks deeply from his bottle, the man from the pages of a magazine with his cover story as bright as mine.

In my experience, the gregarious people are often paddling furiously under the water, and in Guy's case, I know this is true.

CHAPTER FOUR

1. Get a tattoo.
2. Sleep beneath the stars.
3. Visit London.
4. Swim with dolphins.
5. Kiss in the rain.
6. Attend a masquerade ball.
7. Learn to surf.
8. Write and publish a book.
9. Ask a stranger on a date.
10. Fall in love.

I smooth the page I've ripped from my notepad and pin it to the fridge with a round, blue magnet, smiling at the crazy list. Imagine how my prim and proper grandparents would react to some of these. My housemate, Jen, wanders into the kitchen, a wave of floral perfume heralding her arrival.

"Have you seen my phone?" she asks.

Her platinum blonde hair is coiffed into the 1950s style she spends an inordinate amount of time perfecting, face carefully painted to match her image.

"There." I point to the phone half-buried beneath today's mail.

"Thank you!"

Jen's holding a pair of pink heels; her eclectic dress sense reflects her job at a retro boutique nearby. Tonight her outfit consists of tight, black capri pants and a sweetheart neckline, candy pink top.

She drops a matching pink shoe to the ground and slips her foot in. "What do you think of these?" She wiggles her foot.

"Very pretty."

Jen steps forward and peruses my list. "This is interesting. What is it?"

"A bucket list."

"That's so cool! Have you done anything on here yet?" She runs a long fingernail along the paper. "I've done three of these."

"Really?"

She points to her arm where the cartoon-coloured pin-up girl peeks from beneath the cap sleeves of her top. "Several times for some of them! Tattoos, asking guys on dates."

"Do tattoos hurt much?"

"Depends. Why? Is that the first thing you want to do on the list? Start with a small tattoo if you do."

"Start?"

She grabs her phone from the counter. "Oh, yeah, once you've had one tattoo, you'll want more."

Maybe not as many as Jen whose body is covered in a bright inked canvas.

"Almost forgot. You had a call before. I let it ring through to the answer-machine. Why don't you give people your mobile number?"

I can guess who, only one person ever does. "I do, my gran doesn't like calling my mobile."

"Okay. Weird, but fair enough. I'll catch you later." She pauses. "Unless you want to come out this evening?"

"Seeing Cam?"

Jen and Cam, her boyfriend, are normally glued at the hip, their relationship intensifying in the short time I've known them. Some days I wonder why he doesn't move in; he's at the house that often.

"Yeah, but not just him. We're catching up with a few friends for dinner."

"Thanks, but I'm tired."

Jen frowns. "You need to get out more."

"So you keep telling me."

"That should get you out and about." Jen points at the fridge. "But you hardly leave the house apart from work so how the hell are you going to go to London?"

"I'll work up to that one." I turn away, irritated by her judgment. I know I need to make more of a life for myself, but I've no idea how to start. Focusing on making my mark at work takes up my time, success is important, and if I need to stay late to finish up, I do. A social life can wait.

With a shouted goodbye, Jen leaves, the door slamming behind her.

I look at the light blinking on the answer-phone. Why Gran can't use my mobile number, I don't know. Erica does, frequently messaging me and we chat daily. She's concerned, but happier now the new meds are working for me. The dark blanket of sadness has fallen away but the fear is never far, gnawing at the edges of my life, waiting for the chance to slip through.

Uninspired to cook anything else, I pull out last night's leftovers from the fridge, and as I heat the lasagne in the microwave, I read through the page again.

CHAPTER FIVE

#1 *Get a tattoo*

I don't know Guy besides the fact he hangs around suicide spots with bunches of flowers. This is enough to put him in the 'odd' basket in my head, and despite his outward appearance, I don't want Guy to know where I live until I know him better. Instead, on the following Saturday morning, we meet at a car park around the corner from the cafe. I spent the last few evenings researching tattoos, and now I have steeled myself to cross the first item off my list.

Guy's wearing the same clothes as earlier in the week and is paler, eyes rimmed by red.

"Late night?" I ask him.

"Kinda." He twirls his car keys around his finger before clicking the remote. The lights flash on a sporty red Audi and I stop.

"That's your car?"

"Told you I was loaded."

That's the first truth confirmed and the first of my doubts quashed. Perhaps I need to accept he's honest. "Where do you work?"

"I don't. Get in."

People's ability to silence me with short answers is something I need to get a grip on, and learn to push for answers from them. One of the most irritating things in life is coming up with clever retorts several hours too late.

"You have a lot of spare time then."

He frowns. "Phe. That's unkind." I redden and he laughs. "Teasing! I do, but I fill my time with the things I love."

"Surfing?"

"I don't surf."

"But you look like a surfer. And you said you could teach me."

"I mean, I don't surf anymore, a mate got taken by a shark." Guy opens the door and looks across the black soft top of the car at me.

"Oh, my God, really? I'm so sorry!" Guy chews on his lip, fighting a smile. "You're teasing me again, aren't you?"

"Yeah. My mission is to teach you not to let people do that. Don't give people power over you, Phe." He climbs into the car. "I surf. A lot."

When I join him, I'm concerned he'll put the top down; the summer heat has built over the last few days, a true Perth summer gripping the city.

"That's what worries me about surfing. The sharks." *And the water.*

"You'll be in safe hands with me." Guy fires up the engine, loud music instantaneously filling the car. When I blink at the volume, he turns the sound down.

"Why do you want to swim with sharks?" I ask.

"Why do you want to swim with dolphins?"

"Because I've loved them since I was a little girl, we went to Sea World twice and watched the show. At every performance, the handlers pick kids to feed and pet the dolphins, but not me."

"Aww. Poor you," he says and I bristle at his dismissive tone. "I don't like dolphins. I prefer sharks."

"Won't they attack you if you climb in the water with them, though?"

"Nah. I don't taste that good."

I bet he does.

Guy manoeuvres the car onto the street, and turns the music back up, the local chart hits station blasts out ending conversation.

Tucked away on an industrial estate, between an air-conditioning unit distributor and a plumbing warehouse, the skulls on the black painted sign of the small tattoo studio look out of place. Without Guy, I doubt I'd have found this.

Guy climbs out and walks around the side of the car and, before I have a chance to, opens the door for me. "Thanks," I say, surprised by his chivalrous gesture.

After the cool of the car, the humidity washes over me and I'm grateful I wore a short summer dress. Guy scratches his head.

"Where're you having the tattoo?" He indicates the length of my body with his hand. "'Cause you don't want to have to get naked. Shorts and shirt would've been better."

"On my collarbone!" I retort.

"Shame." He strides away.

The fact Guy just implied he wanted to see me naked, momentarily blanks the fear somebody is going to pierce my skin with a multitude of needles.

Inside the studio, photos of clients' tattoos and example art cover the bright red walls. A girl with blue hair and a sleeve of tattoos emerging from her baggy, black t-shirt looks up. "Hey. Got an appointment?"

I clutch my bag, feeling as if I've walked into the waiting room at the doctors, although she's unlike any medical receptionist I've ever seen.

"Hey, Lola. Wes is expecting us," says Guy and indicates me.

Lola flicks me a look. "God, I hope she's not

getting an infinity symbol on her wrist – or a Southern Cross, Wes'll refuse."

"No, *she's* not," I retort.

A middle-aged man with a crew cut appears in the doorway; when he spots Guy, he seizes him in a bear hug. "Hey, mate, how's it going?"

Guy claps him on the back. "Not too bad. Yourself?"

"This the virgin?" Wes asks Guy and looks at me.

Despite strong attempts not to, I turn bright pink. Guy arches a brow.

"Tattoo virgin, I mean," says Wes with a chuckle. "In you go, sweetheart." He gestures to the open door.

"Want me to hold your hand?" asks Guy. "You look pale. Are you worried?"

"No. I'm good."

As I edge past Guy, he leans in. "You never added that to your bucket list," he whispers.

I shiver against his breath tickling my ear. "Added what?"

He steps back and crosses his arms. "V-card, Phe."

"Shut up!" I snap. "Don't make assumptions about me!"

"You're so proper. Do you ever swear? If I were you, I would've told me to fuck off."

I straighten and meet his eyes. "I will if you make any more comments like that."

Guy shakes his head with another smile then turns away. "Hey, Lola. Can you take a look and suggest whereabouts I should put my next tattoo?"

"Take a look where?" she replies, looking up from her phone.

"Wherever you like." He perches on the desk and sweeps a hand, indicating the length of his body.

"Sure, Guy. Why not ask your girlfriend instead?" She points her phone at me.

I wait for Guy's response with interest, but Wes ushers me through a black door before Guy replies.

The couch in Wes's room reminds me of my local GP, grey and covered in white paper. Ohmigod, will I bleed everywhere? The cramped room is covered in more pictures, and there's a small desk holding a large folder and picture frames containing photos of smiling kids.

"You need help choosing?" Wes asks.

This man is an advertisement for his craft, ink spreading across every revealed inch of skin, a mash of colours and pictures that would take a good study to decipher. They stop at his neck, where a red and black skull decorates the front.

"No."

Following the last few evenings searching on the internet, when the design I chose appeared, I knew straightaway I wanted this one. I show Wes the image on my phone. He squints at the picture and groans. "A common one. I got this in my book."

Leaning back in his chair and reaching over his head, he drags a large binder over and opens onto page with artwork of different birds. "Like this?" he asks and points at a series of tiny, black birds in flight.

"Yes, exactly like that."

"Four?"

I nod. They may be cliché, but they mean something to me. Swallowing down my nerves, I eye his tattoo machine in the corner.

"Relax, sweetie, they're small, won't take long."

"Will this be painful?"

"Depends where you're putting it." I brush my fingers along my collarbone to my shoulder and he wrinkles his nose. "Bone. Not promising anything but fleshier is normally easier. Everybody's different though. Let me stencil the design up."

Wes focuses on tracing his drawing while I sit on the edge of the couch and swing my legs. Why did he have to tell me this would hurt? *Of course, having a tattoo will hurt, Phe.*

The noise and vibration is the biggest shock, the needles barely felt. A stinging sensation spreads across my skin. Wes attempts to chat but I switch off, close my eyes, and consider what I'm doing.

All my hopes and plans had been carefully pushed down to the recesses of my mind by the ink black of my thoughts. The four birds flying from the edge of my collarbone to my shoulder represent a freedom from my self-imposed cage. Carving images onto my body mars the perfection I crave, with this tattoo comes a step toward an identity I hide from. Writing a bucket list is an acknowledgement of a future I denied I had, as I sunk beneath the quicksand of my present.

What prompted me to write one? Guy's persistence? Or was each of his nagging texts a reminder I have what he doesn't – a choice to live my life. Again, I drift to thoughts of what's wrong with him. I've never known somebody who is dying – not someone young anyway.

And me. How long will the medication work this time? What if my brain tries to kill me again?

"Done." Wes dabs at my chest with a wet wipe and examines his handiwork before reaching for a mirror. "Here you go."

The reddened skin from the procedure surrounds the small black birds, one flying close to a freckle I never noticed I had there. I didn't take into account how visible this would be. The tattoo won't be covered up in summer clothing and only a few weeks a year in winter jumpers.

Back in the shop, Guy sits on the edge of Lola's desk, chatting. Flirting? Hard to tell, Lola's not responding. I picture her more with a longhaired, biker guy, but who knows? My journalist side goes by the magazine clichés, not always helpful in social situations.

Still, she fights against smiling at whatever joke

he's telling her, Guy's natural charm winning over. But I've seen the depth hidden in his eyes and know beneath he must be struggling to stay afloat.

Shaking my death obsession away, I head over. Guy's eyes zone in on my tattoo.

"Cute ink," he says. "Let's go."

That's it? No praise for my bravery and at starting my bucket list? Irritated, I pay Lola and follow him. Outside, Guy rests against his car with the engine running.

"Lunch?" he asks.

"I have things to do."

"Things?"

"Things." Like, not showing my fresh tattoo to the world just yet.

"You're lying."

"Wow, okay. I'm lying." I climb into the refreshing cool of his car.

Guy hops in next to me. "Come back to mine, I'll make lunch."

His. I absentmindedly touch my freshly scarred skin. "Um."

"Are you worried I'm a stalker? A bit weird?" He starts the car.

Yes. Maybe. "No. I don't know."

Guy tips his head and looks at me in the way that prickles the hairs along my neck because in his eyes rests a connection I deny. "Fair enough. But I did save your life, why would I want to hurt you?"

Uncomfortable with the conversation, I angle the air vents to blow at my stinging skin. "True."

"Just lunch. Nothing else. I promise. I'd like to spend more time with you, that's all."

"Where do you live?"

"Mosman Park."

One of Perth's most expensive suburbs. "Oh. Very nice."

"Yeah, it is. Come take a look."

I scrutinise his face, his expression is friendly but hopeful, putting me in mind of an eager puppy. My life could do with some of his enthusiasm and admittedly, I'm curious about him. I shiver against the cooling temperature as we study each other properly for the first time. One thing's for certain, my elevated heart rate isn't anxiety about being alone with him, but the desire to find out what would happen if I were.

The attraction to Guy built through the texts and his gentle understanding that helped me through the dark times – not just away from the edge of the rocks, at the fact he took time to keep in touch. Now I'm subjected to his physical presence, the draw I have to him intensifies. Do Guy's eyes reflect the same thoughts? Do I want him to?

"I have a few things to do this afternoon. How about I come over this evening?" I suggest.

"Good plan!"

We head away from the industrial estate and back to the suburbs, for the first time, there's a weird tension between us, an awareness of boy meets girl and girl isn't entirely sure of boy's motives.

CHAPTER SIX

I drive to Guy's place, I expected him to live in one of the trendier suburbs, but the surroundings are at odds with his image. A large, ultra-modern house in Mosman Park, amongst the doctors and the self-made millionaires, tucked away on the brow of a hill. Guy wasn't lying; he does have money.

I park halfway down the street, unsure where I'm going and as I stand on the marble porch of the two-storey house, I'm uneasy. Sure, I've met him twice and Guy has secrets, but so do I.

The doorbell echoes through the house and Guy opens one of the glazed double doors. He's relaxed, wearing faded jeans, and a t-shirt covered in streaks of red and blue what looks like paint, feet bare. The dimpled smile gets me every time, as does the awareness of my body's reaction to him. He's beginning to match Ross in my desire for his touch. Not good.

He pads across the shiny, tiled floor and I hesitate before kicking my sandals off and leaving them by the door. A bicycle leans against the wall, dirtying the white paint.

I follow Guy along the hallway, across immaculate, polished marble tiles, paintwork I'm frightened to touch in case I mar with fingerprints. The room opens into a functional but designer kitchen, utensils arranged neatly, hanging from a rack on the wall and stainless steel appliances gleaming.

"Do you live in a show home?" I ask stunned by the lack of empty dishes normally found in the houses of other guys I've known.

"I have a cleaner."

"But still... Do you live on your own?" I hand him the bottle of red wine I brought.

"Yep. How's that tatt?"

I place my fingertips on the ink. He's fielding my questions again. "Fine. Big place to have to yourself."

"I like my own space," he replies. "They look cute on you. You need to tell me who they are."

"Pardon?"

He points at the birds with the bottle. "The birds. There are four. Who are they?"

"Just birds." The look he returns shows he knows I'm lying, this man reads me easily. Guy locates a corkscrew and opens a bottle of red wine. He takes goldfish bowl sized glasses from a glass-fronted cupboard, also finger mark free, and he pours us one each.

Amongst the clean, cool smell of the paint in the house, something is missing. I can't smell food. "What are you cooking?"

"Me? Nothing."

"Oh. You invited me for a meal."

"Yeah." Guy drags a handful of paper menus from the kitchen drawer and drops them on the counter. "What do you like?"

I pick up the first of the array of menus. Thai. Then the next, Chinese. Leafing through I come across Indian, Italian, Vietnamese. "What do you like?" I ask.

"Doesn't matter, you choose."

"I don't care." I push the pile to him.

"Choose." He pushes them back without a glance.

"Honestly, I don't mind."

Guy rests against the counter, and crosses his arms. "Phe, make decisions."

"I do! I just don't care what I eat."

"Then we don't eat." Guy gulps back his wine.

Uncomfortably, I shift, debating whether to leave. "Seriously, I don't care."

"If you were on your own, you'd choose what you want. Don't worry about what I want."

"I'm not!" I shake my head at him. "Normally, when I go around to someone's place for dinner, they cook."

"I can cook if you like."

"I didn't mean that."

Guy pulls out three menus and lines them up. "These are my favourites. I'll compromise. Choose one and I'll decide what we eat."

"You're weird. Fine."

Following the altercation over meals, Guy orders. When the Chinese food arrives, he tips the contents of the containers into large, white serving bowls. Beneath the bright spotlights in his kitchen, on stools at the counter, isn't the most romantic of meals, but this could be why Guy chose the location. Am I misreading his interest?

"Why did you make such a big deal out of that?" I ask.

"I think you need to learn to be more assertive. I get the impression people make decisions for you a lot." He mixes rice with the chicken and black bean sauce. "Am I right?"

"I'm not naturally pushy, but I can stand up for myself, thanks."

"No, but you're not as confident as you pretend."

I poke at the meal. "You don't know what I'm

like."

"I know that you probably do what people expect of you so you can avoid conflict."

"Are you a psychologist or something?"

Guy shakes his head. "No."

"What do you do?"

"I told you before. Nothing." He tops up the wine glasses. "You?"

"I write for a magazine." Funny how we've spoken about everything and nothing.

"That's right! You never told me which one, though."

"*Belle de Jour.*"

His mouth twitches as he fights a smile. "Serious?"

"What's funny?"

"The kinds of articles in those kinds of magazines... I can't picture you writing them. Surely, you don't buy into all that bullshit. Perfect life, perfect body, perfect sex life?"

I switch my focus to the rice, discussing sex with Guy causes images to emerge that in turn cause aching I don't need. "No."

"Not a very healthy environment for somebody like you."

We remain in silence until I realise he's skirted around my question. "What do you mean you don't do anything?"

"I don't work."

"You have money though. This place is very nice."

"I do have money, too much. Inheritance."

"Right."

"So, I'm living what's left of my life until it catches up again."

The vagueness of 'it' tempts me to ask what he means, but I'm unsure I should. Guy's right, I need to work on my assertiveness.

"What do you do all day then?"

"Live my life. Some days I like being outdoors: surf, walk, whatever." He points at the ceiling with his fork. "Other days I stay inside all day. Paint."

"You're an artist? That explains your t-shirt." I indicate the smudges and now I'm closer I can see light blue smears on his arms.

"Am I? Not really. Nobody ever taught me, I just like to paint sometimes. Empties my head."

"Can I see what you paint?"

"No."

I blink at his abruptness and Guy indicates my tattoo. "You were going to tell me who they are."

I touch the black birds. "How do you know they represent people?"

"I don't, just a guess."

I inhale and hold the breath, which is a mistake because lack of oxygen spins me back to that night. "My parents and brother. And me."

"What do you think your parents will say about the tattoo? Are they old fashioned?"

I clear my throat. "They're dead."

Guy blinks several times. "Sorry to hear that."

"My brother too."

"Shit, sorry. Accident?"

"Can I not talk about this, Guy?" I whisper. Too late, the dreams will return tonight. I know from the tightening head and shortening breath that the images will follow. At least the tears don't come anymore.

"I lost my family, too," he says.

"I'm sorry."

Guy shrugs. "Life goes on."

The connotations of his words hang heavily between us: apart from when life doesn't.

We share the bottle of wine, chat about movies we like, books we've read, anything but each other. Guy steers the conversation to neutral territory, keeping us above the water and not looking at what lies beneath. I relax, he's the kind of person who makes poor jokes, his sense of humour as odd as the rest of him, but I'm convinced he's harmless.

"Should we discuss the next item on the list?" he asks.

"It's your turn to choose."

"You still need to catch up. Another one of yours."

I picture the list attached to my fridge by a magnet. "I'm not sure."

"How about 'Ask a stranger on a date?' That one's easy and inexpensive," he suggests.

I fiddle with the edge of my sleeve, why does he have to keep mentioning that one? I'm also annoyed I'm projecting a fantasy of a secret romance onto Guy when he's clearly not interested. "Maybe."

"There must be somebody you can ask. If you're lucky you might end up doing your tenth."

"Tenth?"

"'Fall in love'. The item at the end of your list."

I laugh. "I'm sure if the guy knew that, he'd run a mile. 'Hello, do you want to go on a date and then we can fall in love?'"

"Meh. Just tell him about your list. Ice-breaker."

"Smart."

"I sure am."

We share a relaxed smile, surprised by how easily our text message based relationship has translated into face to face. As he clears the plates away, I watch Guy's lithe movements. The muscles move in Guy's back against his t-shirt as he stacks plates in the dishwasher, and the thought of touching him creeps in again. This isn't helped when he sits back down close to me, placing his arms on the kitchen counter. His hands are slender, blue paint stuck beneath his nails.

The awareness of Guy as a man, not the random stranger who hangs around cliff tops with bunches of flowers confuses me. This is a friendship. Travelling companions. Nothing more. He just proved that by talking to me about asking another person on a date.

"Are you okay?" he asks.

I look into the eyes that remind me of the water that almost drowned me, at the concern set in his brow. His dimples are childish marks that are at odds with his very grown-up aura. "Do you have a girlfriend?" I ask.

He arches a brow. "Why? Are you volunteering?"

Something new passes between us, clarifying the situation. Guy feels this too, the pull between us. I swallow. "No. I'm not looking for a boyfriend. Not at the moment."

"Falling in love is on my list, too, if I had a girlfriend that one would be ticked off. I guess I need to find somebody."

"You can have a girlfriend and not be in love."

"What would be the point in that?"

"Men often have girlfriends and aren't in love."

The amused curve appears on his lips again. "And girls don't?"

"Not as much, I think they expect a great love."

"Do you?"

"Not really."

Guy swirls the wine remaining in his glass then drinks. "Don't wait your whole life for a Prince Charming to bring you a happy ever after, find your own."

"I intend to."

"Good. The only person who can make you complete is yourself."

I drain my glass. "You're a strange person."

"Better than being something I'm not. No pigeon holes for me."

Does he hide his pain as well as I do? I've almost asked him several times this evening what's wrong with him, but can't. I refused to open up about the pain behind my illness. I can't expect him to open up to me.

"I've had an idea," says Guy, topping up our glasses. "I honestly think we should do the lists together. All of them."

"I already said I was fine with that."

"I know, but plan things. One every week or so for the items on the lists we can do nearby. Meet up, have fun for a few hours, and then back to reality. No strings. No expectations." I sip my wine and study him over the rim. No expectations. Can I spend time with Guy and not want more? Is that what he's hinting at? Casual hook-ups to accompany our weird dates? *Dates?*

"How long for?" I ask. "I mean, how long do you have?"

He remains looking at me then rubs his head. "A few months."

"Can I ask what's wrong with you?"

He sighs and puts down his glass. "No. I will tell you, but not yet. I don't want to spoil our evening."

"Oh. Right. Sorry I didn't mean to cause you issues."

"All good, Phe."

We haven't moved from the kitchen and my back aches from sitting too long in the low backed stool. "I should go. I'm tired."

Guy slides his phone across the bench and checks the time. "Eleven. You okay to drive home?"

"I'm fine. I've only had a couple of glasses. Thanks for the meal."

"Thanks for choosing." I pout at him and he laughs. "Catch up soon?"

"When I find something on the list?"

"If you like." Guy stands too. "Can I ask one more question?"

"Okay..." I'd hoped to leave before the awkward goodbye joined us. I can't help feel the conversations

51

around 'fun' had deeper connotations, or that Guy notices my attraction to him. He hasn't stood this close to me since the night we met. When we sat together, there was a distance, now almost face to face that's closed again. He rubs a finger along his lips as he studies me and I'm increasingly convinced the attraction is mutual.

"What's Phe short for if your name isn't Fiona?"

I take a shaky breath, caught off guard. "Ophelia, but nobody calls me that. Ever."

He shrugs. "No problem, I was curious because I've never met a Phe before."

"I've never met a Guy before."

"Not one like me, that's for sure." The conversation remains light but the tension weighs heavy between us. Oh, yeah, definitely not one like you. I've never met a man who jump-starts my heart every time his dark blue eyes meet mine.

I keep my cool and hope he doesn't notice my reaction. "Undoubtedly."

He shifts closer and I will him not to touch me, and wish he would. "Bye, Ophelia. Keep your head above the water."

The name washes over, pulling me back to the past and wiping away the present. This breaks the tensions and makes leaving easier, and following a muttered goodbye, I head outside into the fresh air.

Guy doesn't understand what his words have done and what I'm facing tonight.

CHAPTER SEVEN

Water fills the car. I managed to crank open the door a small amount as we plunged beneath the river, panic prompting me to choose the wrong choice of action. The car was afloat after it hit the river but when I opened the door, the flooding water hastened the submersion.

My parents don't move, and I scream for them as the pressure slams the door closed again. My little brother, Robin, doesn't wake, strapped in his car seat and sleeping. I fumble with the buckle, gasping for air in the waterlogged space. My head dips beneath the water, muffling my cries for help as I struggle to unstrap him.

Darkness engulfs, the water stealing my family one by one. I unclip my brother and desperately hold Robin in the small air space above the water. I can't get us out of the car and hold him up at the same time. The door won't open against the pressure of the water; I kick at the window but my bare feet do nothing.

My screams are swallowed by the water, stealing my world and my life. Eleven years old is too young to die.

I slam my hands on the window, the air bubbling from my nose to the glass as the water consumes the last of the air.

Heaving a breath, I sit, heart skipping in my chest and I close my eyes again. I'm not dying. I'm not having a heart attack. I can breathe. The light at the side of my bed illuminates my room, and I ground myself by counting the photo frames on the top of my chest of drawers. For a few moments, I sit with my arms wrapped around my legs before I'm calm enough to lie down again. The lamp casts a shadow across the wall. I never sleep in the dark anymore.

The thoughts are back to torture me, the nightly replay of the night my father killed everybody I loved begins again.

CHAPTER EIGHT

"Can I touch?"

Erica doesn't wait for a response, instead lightly running a finger across the shiny black ink against my pale skin. The tattoo healed and, a week later, somebody from my past sees.

"When did you do that? Why didn't you tell me you were getting a tattoo? This isn't like you!" She streams out the words in shock.

"It's on my bucket list."

"You have a bucket list?"

"Doesn't everyone?"

Erica sits on the sofa in my bright and airy lounge. "I have things I want to do, but not an actual list. You wrote them down?"

"Yes. Don't you have one?"

"A vague one. Should've expected you'd be all organised. I bet you have deadlines for each one too."

I poke my tongue out. "Do you want me to take you for lunch or not?"

"Yeah, to that coffee shop where the guy works you told me about. Mr Eyelashes."

"What a weird thing to call him."

"You mentioned his eyelashes! I mean, come on, that's not the part of his body where length matters."

"Erica!"

She grins. "Legs! He has to be taller than you! Whatever did you think I meant?"

"Sure," I mutter, "let me grab my bag."

Friends since high school, Erica's candy bright attitude to the world smudges colour over my grey. I owe Erica for helping me through my teen years, growing up with grandparents after the loss of my family and a switch of towns and schools no doubt triggered the dark side of my mind. My friendship with Erica stopped the depression blacking me completely.

Erica follows me into my bedroom. "How are the new meds going?" she asks.

The box rests at the edge of my bedside table and I quickly push them into a drawer. "Better."

"You worry me. I wish I lived closer for when you needed me."

"I'm fine, Erica. The change in meds a few months back screwed with my head. I don't have the thoughts anymore."

Erica has seen through my lies before and I'm thankful she wasn't around at the time I met Guy. His daily texts and calls after the day I almost died prompted me to see my doctor, keep going with the medication, and hold me in a world I fought against.

In the early days, the change in medication screwed with my ability to think, walking around in a leaden-limbed daze that took me away from the thoughts instead of dealing with them. Gradually, I moved from not seeing a future to the prodding by Guy to create one. Guy's background presence stopped me turning back into the shadows; now I've allowed him to pull me into the bright future he's being denied.

"A bucket list is good though, tells me you're thinking of the future."

Erica doesn't know. Nobody knows apart from Guy and my psychiatrist. The day after I met Guy, I saw my psychiatrist and admitted to him that I had thoughts about harming myself. Guy texted to check up on me and I informed him I was being admitted to hospital. I debated whether to give Guy my number the night we met and there's a deep-seated reason why I did. By doing so, I made myself accountable to Guy. The texts continued. On days I didn't reply, Guy would send funny memes until I'd relent and respond. I can only cope with a finite number of funny cat pictures in one day.

"I should write one too, just things like places I want to visit. Not a tattoo though." Erica shakes her head. "Still can't believe you did that!"

"I might not stop at one."

I'm half-serious.

We head to the city, despite the fact I prefer to stay out of the place at weekends, but Erica's flown from Melbourne to visit and she wants to compare Perth to our home. She was horrified when I chose to move to the loneliest city in the world, isolating myself the same way Perth is. Perth is more than 2500 miles to the nearest Australian city. I'd hoped moving would help, not appreciating that even though the stress was good because I got the job I wanted, the relocation still had an effect on me. I underestimated the strength of my pull to the familiarity of friends and family. But I'm stronger than I thought and I'm pulling through. Slowly.

"Which one?" Erica asks.

I indicate the small shop tucked between a real estate agent and a bookshop. "There isn't much room!"

"The place is more coffee shop than cafe."

"Evidently" She wrinkles her nose and sits, pulling a face at the crumbs left on the table by previous occupants.

I check out the staff behind the long, marble counter and spot Ross. Immediately, I duck my head. I'd hoped he wouldn't be here because Erica is bound to say something I'm sure will call me out.

"I'll buy the coffees! What would you like?" I ask.

"Vanilla latte." She doesn't look up from the menu.

Ross is serving another customer, so I'm served by somebody else, and avoid another attempt to hide my attraction to him, deliberately not looking in his direction. When I return to the table, Erica's smirk says everything.

"That's him." She sucks the froth from her spoon and indicates Ross.

"Shush!" I grab her hand.

"Why sit so you can hardly see him? You could flirt with him from here."

"I don't want to flirt with him!"

"Jeez, I would." She sips from her cup. "But, out of respect to you, I won't."

Erica loves to flirt, and especially enjoys shooting down in flames anybody who hits on her in an obnoxious way. She's half a foot shorter than I am, complains she's average everything; but Erica is also a master of disguise and has an impressive array of make-up and clothes. Her hair is currently blonde; last time I saw her, it was as brown as mine. One thing's certain; Erica's never short of attention.

I tear open a sugar sachet and tip the contents into my coffee. "I don't want to get involved with somebody."

"A date or two wouldn't hurt."

At school, I didn't bother with boyfriends, instead spending all my time studying. Same when I went to uni. Sure, I had boyfriends and went through the whole relationship make and break cycle once with a guy from my creative writing class, then gave up. Luckily, I got bored before he did. Battling the dark moods was enough, facing more relationship breakdowns would have added to the spiral.

"How's the job? Any better?" asks Erica.

I've whinged to Erica plenty of times, my excitement over the role tempered within weeks, thanks to my treatment by the boss. Did Pam have the same baptism of fire when she started out? I haven't figured Pam's age yet or the trajectory her career took but she seems to think being a bitch is acceptable people management.

"I'm not sure Pam thinks I can do the job."

"Of course you can! Don't let somebody ruin what you want to achieve. Just don't stay if the job's making you unhappy, it's not worth the stress. You can always look for another job and you'll have experience."

"How's life as a post-grad?" I reply.

"Good. Stop changing the subject."

"I hope you didn't come over here to mother me."

"Fine!"

My phone beeps and I pull it from under Erica's in case I miss a message from work.

"Hey! We said no phones while we're chatting!" She takes the phone from me and looks at the screen. "Who's Guy?" Erica looks up from the message.

"Just some Guy," I say with a smile to myself.

"Some significant Guy?"

God, I hope the message is a sane one.

"'Hey, beautiful. Check this out'," reads Erica. "Um. Beautiful?"

I snatch the phone away. "He's a friend."

"How come you never mentioned him? How long have you known him?"

"About three months."

"Three months? Far out! Who is he?"

How do I explain Guy to Erica? Or anyone? He hovers on the fringes of my life because I won't let him in. Since I got the tattoo and spent the evening with him a couple of weeks ago, we've conversed by text only; he never tries to call. Is he waiting for me to contact him first?

I click on the link and the webpage opens to a charity masquerade ball being held in Perth in a couple of weeks. I was aware, invites were emailed to work, but huge social events with an expectation of networking don't appeal.

"Like I said, just a casual friend. We've only met a couple of times."

Erica points at my phone. "Photo? Is he hot?"

"I guess..."

"Photo!" She grabs the phone from me and scrolls through my pictures. "Huh. Why no picture? Facebook? Is he on there?" She clicks open the app.

"No idea, I never asked."

"You're friends but not Facebook friends. That's weird."

"Not really, I just don't know him well."

"Well enough for him to call you beautiful!"

"I don't think he reserves that term for me only."

"So what did he message about?"

"Nothing." I switch my phone off and place it pointedly on the table.

Erica eyes my shaking hand. "Is he a creeper? Is that the problem?"

"No, no." How do I explain this? "We're friends. We're... working on our bucket lists together."

Erica sits back. "What does that involve?"

"So far, not much. We're planning what to do."

"Phe, do you know how weird that sounds? Kinda romantic too."

"No romance."

"So Mr Eyelashes is in with a chance? Two men to choose from!"

"Erica!"

I look over my shoulder. Ross serves a new customer adding his natural charm to the order, broad smiles for the young mother and her brown-haired daughter. Ross remembers the names of regulars, asks how their day is with genuine interest; I've heard him many times. I stare, as I often do, picturing his full lips on mine, his large hands against my skin.

'Ask a stranger on a date'?

Ross looks over, because he has a sixth sense I'm staring or because he noticed where I sat when I arrived here? Our eyes meet briefly, too brief to gauge any interest.

No, I'm one of hundreds of customers who pass through here daily. Part of Ross's job is to keep customers coming back and flirting is a useful tool to use. Rejection would be embarrassing. I need to choose somebody who I'm certain is interested.

****

I responded to Guy's text with an "I'll think about it" and he didn't reply. That was two days ago.

He's a curious person, sometimes his texts are sharp and witty, smoothing the rough edges off frustrating days, and other times they're short and opinionated. This dichotomy puts me off. I'm uncomfortable spending time with people who I'm unsure how they will react. I like my world organised and predictable; people who aren't don't fare well in my life.

I return to work refreshed after my weekend with Erica. Today, Pam is out interviewing a local doctor who's an ambassador for women, the type of woman who stands for the person I'd like to be when I'm older: successful, self-assured, and an achiever. I'm left to copy edit articles and scour stock photo sites for suitable accompanying shots. An hour later, and my eyes glaze as I stare at beautiful beaches and tropical paradises. The untouched sand and solitude would add these places to anybody's bucket list, why aren't they on mine? Because I live in a city edged by impossibly blue ocean and white sands, my preference is to experience the cold and rugged.

And I hate water.

I'd like to visit historical places. England. With my bucket list partner. Possibly.

My phone beeps. <Are you coming to the ball, Cinderella? I need to know>

Guy texts the link again and I glance around before clicking on the invite. My experience of balls is school formals. One school formal. A childish excitement harking back to childish dreams of being a princess accompany as I read the description and look at the photos. Ball gowns and beautiful people, mysterious Prince Charmings. I shake my head, well aware the thrill of disguise underlies the attraction of masquerade balls.

What would Guy look like in a suit? The image amuses me – the raw material of the casual Guy unimaginable in formal attire. Undoubtedly hot though. I dismiss the thought, Guy's not interested in me, and we know too much about what's wrong with each other.

<Okay> I reply.

<Excellent>

I smile at the text and return to the stock photo site and somehow find myself on Etsy, because going to a masquerade ball calls for research, obviously.

CHAPTER NINE

#6 *Attend A Masquerade Ball*

As a girl, I loved Cinderella. Absolutely adored the story, spent weeks with my head filled with the tale of the downtrodden girl and the handsome prince. My mum got sick of watching the Disney movie on repeat while I flounced around the house in a blue dress and tiara. Secretly, I wanted to be the fairy godmother because she could perform magic – I had plans for my cat that may or may not have involved dress-ups.

Then, one day I read the Brothers Grimm version of the fairy tale in which the ugly sisters cut off parts of their feet to fit into the glass slipper. The victim of an overactive imagination my whole life, this gave me nightmares for a week. That was the end of my love affair with Cinderella and all Disney princesses. Who knows what horrors lie in the other books?

This doesn't stop me spending the next two weekends shopping for a dress any princess would be jealous of. Masquerade balls hold mystery and allure, a step out of reality and back in time. Eventually, I find a dress I can't really afford. The dress hugs my hips, reaching the floor. The gathered gold bodice pushes my not very ample breasts upward so I look several sizes bigger, pulling in my waist to give me a classic hourglass figure. Silver thread runs from the seam, across the dress, and curling across one side of the bodice, sparkling like stars when the dress moves and catches the light. The shoes match perfectly, black and gold, adding several inches to my height. I spent an hour in the shop justifying buying everything. I told myself this is my bucket list and I should let go of the constraints I attach to myself, financial or otherwise

Choosing a mask was fun, I spent hours on Etsy looking for something different, and eventually, chose a Venetian gold butterfly mask where one eye spreads upwards in a butterfly shape, the wings touching the side of my pinned-up hair.

The evening of the ball, when I prepare to leave the house, Cam and Jen are in the lounge watching TV. Jen had helped me into the dress and enthused about the fit and quality, bemoaning the fact she couldn't borrow it due to our height and build difference. Her track pants and oversized blue shirt are about as far removed from my outfit as you can find.

Cam stares as I walk in to say my goodbyes, rendered speechless for a moment. I place my phone into my gold bag then pick up the mask, avoiding his eyes.

I like Cam; he's friendly and tempers Jen's exuberance with his calm nature. Into the same scene as her, Cam has tattoos beneath his vintage black shirt and brown hair slicked upwards in a pompadour style. He's a few years older than her, one of those people you can't quite tell how much older. Cam's maturity outweighs Jen's by at least ten years. Perhaps that's unfair, Jen likes to live life and screw the consequences. She runs out of money within days of being paid, her wardrobe brimming with clothes, and has no thought for the long-term, whereas I'm all for career paths and superannuation.

"Looking good," says Cam. "Lucky guy."

"Guy?"

"The guy you're going with, he won't be able to keep his hands off you, I'll bet." Jen purses her lips at Cam, increasing my discomfort. "What? She's stunning, but what chick wouldn't be dressed up like that."

"I wish we were going," says Jen, placing her legs across his lap.

"Yeah, waste of money, babe."

"The ball is for charity," I reply.

"We don't have money to throw at charities." He nods. "But have fun."

Guy bought the tickets, with his usual protest that he had the money, and if he was going to take a girl to a ball, he should pay. I relented to his old-fashioned view. Cam's comment about Guy not wanting to keep his hands off me sticks. Does that concern or excite me? I push the thought away.

The masquerade ball is held at the most expensive hotel in the city, one recently refurbished to rival the most exclusive establishments in Sydney or Melbourne. Their sponsorship of the event ensures this new image will receive a lot of attention. The taxi drops me at the marble-pillared entrance where I make my way through the other arrivals and into the building.

The vast modern lobby is filled with chattering groups, voices amplified by the high ceilings. The hotel is an eclectic mix of traditional and modern, the dark grey painted feature walls at odds with the unusually shaped chandelier above. I agreed to meet Guy close to the entrance; but now I'm here, I wish we'd arrived together.

Finding Guy could prove difficult. Every man here is hidden by a mask and many wear identical dress suits and are only distinguishable by their build. I've never seen Guy in a suit and can't imagine him in one, add in the mask and he'll be impossible to spot. I should've asked him to pick me up from home.

Initially, I take quick glances nearby men in case

he's one of them, but become uncomfortable they'll think I'm checking them out and using my mask as an excuse. What else can I do but appraise their height and build to figure out if any of them is Guy? I'm not interested in faceless men.

A stressful ten minutes later, and the only solution is to text Guy. A sick worry he might not arrive at all grips me as I begin a message. Half way through typing, my screen flashes with a picture of myself taken recently. The mask fortunately obscures the panic but I'm secretly pleased by how I look. The view in the mirror before left me feeling over-dressed and awkward; the poised girl in the picture stands out amongst the guests around her.

<Looking good, Belle>

I glance in the direction I imagine the picture was taken from and a group stand in the open doorway to the function room, chatting. No Guy.

<Where are you?>

<Look again>

A man sidesteps the group and heads toward me. I recognise Guy's gait but until he reaches me, he's indiscernible from the crowd. Guy's white mask obscures half his face, but his strong jaw and full mouth are visible still. The well-cut black suit jacket is unbuttoned, a grey shirt with bow tie beneath.

Guy looks a hell of a lot hotter out of his boardies and the control over my attraction to him loosens further.

A low whistle accompanies Guy's appraisal of me. "You scrub up well."

"Nicely put. You're not quite Prince Charming then?"

"Not if you're Belle." He crooks his elbow indicating I should place my arm through his.

"Belle?"

"You're wearing gold which is closer to yellow. Beauty and the Beast."

"I'd hardly call you a beast." I hesitate over

whether to take his arm or not.

"There are so many inappropriate responses I can give to that comment and won't." He pauses. "I've told you before, you're beautiful."

I blush like a teenager beneath my mask and heavy make-up. "Thanks."

"Not just tonight," he says softly.

I hastily change the subject. "You look very different in a suit."

"Devastatingly sexy?"

"I was going to go with 'good'." *Yes, and you know you are.*

"'Good'? Not even hot? Seriously?"

"I'm never sure whether you're serious and in love with yourself, or if you're joking."

"Ah, a bit of both." He gestures again for me to take his arm.

We touch.

Every day I touch new people. Shake hands with clients, am jostled by people on the way to and from work, but until now I didn't realise I've avoided touching Guy. When we first met, his touch would've pulled me away from the edge and taken away control of my body and decisions.

As I link my arm through Guy's, a finality strikes, too. The distance I've tried to maintain, the illusion our only connection is a night of my life I refuse to see as part of myself, retreats as we connect. His arm is warm against my bare skin and the curve of his bicep beneath the expensive suit doesn't escape my attention either. Caught in the romance of the setting, the nervous fluttering in my stomach switches to desire for Guy's touch. I resolve to limit the amount of alcohol and physical contact for the evening.

Six glasses of champagne later, this plan fails. We sit at a large, round table covered by a floor length white cloth. In front are nameplates, metal centrepieces of gold painted flowers surrounded by wrapped chocolates. The hundred or so tables are spaced around the huge room and face the stage where a burlesque show plays out.

Everybody at our table keeps their masks on, and this doesn't encourage conversation. Many tables are groups who've come together; the other five people at our table are a party from a legal firm, so our conversation with them barely moves beyond pleasantries.

The food served is curious looking hors d'oeuvre only. I forgot to eat with my focus on getting ready tonight. A decent loading of carbs before I left home would've been sensible, because the ability of sparkling wine to enter my bloodstream quickly is apparent by my loosening tongue.

"How do you know so much about Disney princesses?" I ask Guy. "I doubt many men would know the different princess's colours."

"My sister loved Disney princesses and Belle was her favourite." He sips his wine.

"I liked Cinderella."

"Interesting." I glance at him for a teasing smile, but he's serious. "Does that mean I get to be Prince Charming after all?"

"I thought you said I was Belle."

He taps the table and I wait for another Beast comment, but none comes.

The burlesque girls swing across the stage on decorated trapezes, descending from the ceiling in the blue glow of the stage lights. I never understood how burlesque could be any more than arty stripping, but the show refutes that. These women are in control, both of their performance and the crowd. These women don't subscribe to the crazy fad diets my employers tout; costumed in corsets and lace, they own their sexuality rather than playing to a false ideal.

"Can you dance?" asks Guy.

Our masks remain in situ, the illusion more

exciting than I'd imagined. I'm somebody else tonight, disguised and free. There are people here I recognise but the mask allows me to pretend I don't notice them, further on the edge of the small world of the Perth media and marketing.

"Dancing? Depends what kind," I reply.

"I suspect something more formal and less Gangnam style."

An image of Guy dancing that way amuses me and I giggle. "That's so 2012, Guy."

He runs a finger around the rim of his wine glass. "Ah, so she does laugh, and such a sound it is too."

"Of course I laugh!"

"Then I'm happy because this means you're a step further away from the edge," he whispers.

With Guy, I am a step away. In an odd way, he represents a future I never considered, even though he won't be in mine for long.

I hesitate when the couples take to the dance floor, folding and unfolding the napkin on my lap and avoiding Guy's eyes. I can wear my confidence as a mask; but when I'm in new situations, I can't pretend. One thing I hate is making an idiot of myself. Failing. The last time I formally danced was at my Year 12 ball, where I experienced awkward moments with boys from school who decided ass groping was the height of seduction.

Guy will ask me to dance and we'll stand close. The thought fires anticipation over what will happen once my whole body touches his.

"I can't tell beneath the mask, but I suspect you're worrying. Please laugh again," Guy says.

"You'll be the one laughing if you try dancing with me in these shoes."

"Belle, you cannot come to a masquerade ball and not dance. I refuse to let you cross this off your list unless you dance at least once." Guy stands and extends an open hand. "Come on. Relax. Nobody can see you. Let that fun girl out for the evening. I know she's in there."

One dance, my hormones can cope with that, surely.

The couples on the dancefloor move harmoniously to the gentle sound of the waltz, the women in elegant dresses and their gentlemanly, restrained dance partners create a step back in time. I join Guy at the edge of the floor; and when we face each other, I wish his face wasn't obscured by the white mask, so I could read him. "You look like the Phantom of the Opera."

"Love that musical. Not sure whether I like the comparison though."

Surfer Guy likes musicals and art? "Right."

A woman in a scarlet red dress sweeps by, her partner leading her across the floor in a graceful movement I doubt I'll be able to emulate. Before I can comment, Guy circles my waist and pulls me close, taking my hand in his. This is closer than I intended. I didn't think this through. He's careful not to draw me too near, but his warmth and strength is apparent even with the gap between us. Guy's firm grip contrasts his soft hands as he guides me into the dancers.

In my heels, I'm close to his face and even in the dim, and half-hidden, the sculpted curves of his face and generous mouth paint his beauty. I hesitate, and then place a hand on his back. He's jacket-less and the strong sinew of the muscles beneath his shirt strikes me. As my head moves closer to his, I catch his scent of spice and the ocean, the one behind his eyes.

"See. You can dance," says Guy as he guides me around the dance floor.

In response, I trip over his feet. "If you don't remind me and let me go with the flow, your feet will survive."

"Fine." He hasn't pulled his gaze from mine the whole time, this connection drawing us further into the dance. We naturally follow each other's movements, as if we've done this a hundred times before.

As the dance progresses, Guy holds me closer, until the last of the space between us disappears.

He doesn't react but my body does, a sudden heat flowing from the point his fingertips touch the naked skin on my arms, kindling the desire to dig my fingers into his back further. If I keep my eyes on Guy's, I can stay grounded, ignore the hidden strength of the raw man beneath his cultured exterior, and dismiss the images of what he could do to me.

Shocked but not entirely surprised when my nipples harden against my bodice, accompanied by a not very chaste tingling elsewhere, I break the point chests touch. Guy doesn't comment or stop; he continues and loosens his hold on my waist.

"Sorry," he whispers against my ear as I move my head to look past him. This unfortunately brings my face closer to his, the side of our unmasked faces brush. I jerk at the sensation.

"What for?"

"Getting too close."

"We're dancing. I'm fine."

"Do you want to stop?" Guy's warm breath caresses my cheek, nose touching my ear, and I'm on the verge of twisting my face to gauge if a kiss is next.

Is this what I want?

I disentangle myself. "My feet are starting to hurt."

"Right."

"And I'm tired."

The side of Guy's face I can see shifts into concerned lines. "Everything okay?"

"I think so."

We head through the dancing bodies to the table; I sit and pour myself water from the half-empty carafe. Although neither of us speaks, the awareness the dance has somehow shifted our relationship hovers in the charged air between us. Confused by what I really want from the situation, and aware I have work tomorrow, I resolve to keep the line between us uncrossed.

"Am I allowed to tick this off my list now?" I ask.

"You danced. Putting yourself through that trauma deserves a tick."

"Dancing wasn't traumatic!" I say with a laugh.

"But you stopped. Did I make you uncomfortable?"

Quite the opposite. "You're a good dance partner. You didn't grope my ass so that was a bonus."

The dimples appear again. "I have a lot of self-restraint. Your ass is very gropeable."

"Nice."

He shrugs. "Hey, I'm a man and you're an attractive girl."

My fingers itch to take his mask off and see the expression behind his words, to find if my desire is reflected in his eyes. "Thanks."

"This is the part where you tell me I'm 'hot', exchange of compliments, remember?"

"You don't need me to tell you that."

"Very true. I hope you're not thinking of leaving soon. I'm enjoying this and I've even spotted you beginning to relax."

"You're good company."

He laughs. "And you're so formal!"

"But I'm not sure I'll stay much longer, sorry."

Guy shakes his wrist to read his watch. "You *are* Cinderella not Belle. And you're late, it's twelve thirty."

"Ha ha. You stay if you want."

"What point is the prince without the princess?"

"You're not a prince, you're just some Guy."

I giggle again; but instead of laughing with me, Guy's mouth twitches. "Okay, let's go."

He stands and knocks his chair back then strides away. That was a joke, he makes them enough, why be offended by mine? I hurry to catch up, weaving through the half-empty tables and into the shining hotel lobby where other guests mill around. The music from the function room is replaced by the sound of one couple arguing at an uncomfortable volume nearby.

"I'll call a taxi, we can share one?" I suggest as I reach Guy.

"Which direction do you live in?"

"Leederville."

"Wrong way for me, but I'll come with you, make sure you're in the taxi safely," he offers.

"I'm fine."

"Suit yourself."

The atmosphere has dropped to several degrees below zero and I'm unsure why. I thought our exchange was banter. Guy buries his hands in his jacket pockets and heads outside as I call the taxi, wandering to the large sliding glass doors and watching him as I make the call.

Guy perches on a wall at the edge of the pick-up area outside the lobby, hands in his pockets, and mask still on.

"Five minutes," I say as I approach.

"Okay."

I sit next to him. "Did I annoy you?"

"Annoy me? No, I was having fun, that's all. But I understand if you've had enough."

"I enjoyed myself. Honestly."

The arguing couple head past, and when the woman trips and lands on the floor, the man stands and looks down at her, arms crossed.

"I thought maybe because you'd rather be here with someone else," he says quietly.

"No, you're my travelling companion. Who else would I bring? Complete the lists together, remember?"

His shoulders relax and he shifts, our legs touching. The summer evening is muggy, no breeze to cool my skin heated by the dance. Guy looks upwards where the Southern Cross shines brightly in the cloudless sky. "Shame. I wish it was raining."

"You'd rather wait in the rain?" I ask in surprise.

Guy smiles beneath his mask and keeps his gaze on the stars. "Your list. Number five. As your travelling companion, I'd be happy to oblige."

Kiss in the rain.

My heart skips at his directness. "You want to kiss me?" I whisper.

"Purely for bucket list purposes."

"Take your mask off." Guy unties the mask and slides it from his face. His hair sticks up on one side and I study him. I need to know the truth behind Guy's words and the situation.

"That's the only reason?" I ask.

Guy reaches to touch my cheek, drawing a finger along to my jaw, watching the path it takes before looking back to me. "No."

The sensation of his finger remains when he removes his hand, and I fight and fail against appearing to be a stupefied teen. "Oh."

"You don't want to?"

I shift my leg away from his. "Might not be a good idea."

"Why?"

"I'm not sure… It's just…" I grapple for words. "I like being friends." As soon as the lie is out, I cringe.

Guy purses his lips, his disappointment clear. "I suspected so. You're very protective."

"Cold?"

"Protective." He folds his arms beneath his elbows. "Is one of the reasons because there's somebody else?"

"I told you there wasn't."

"Is the reason because I'm going to die?"

I reel at the interjection of death into our conversation, but Guy's face is impassive. The words are nothing to him. "No. Not unless my kiss will kill you."

"Maybe your kiss would do the opposite." I attempt to equate the man sitting with me to the casual Aussie bloke who took me for a tattoo, and realise I forget the depth in his eyes.

"Most guys – men – don't ask permission before trying their luck," I say with a small smile.

He laughs. "I think you want to kiss me too, but I think sometimes, the princess should call the shots."

"You're putting me in control of this?" I ask and stand.

Guy stands too and looks down at me. He slides my mask upward, into my hair. "To a certain extent, yes." He rests his fingertips on my lips, and I shiver. "But I like to be in control as much as you do."

"Some things we can't control, can we?"

"Some things we think we need to when letting go is better." He shifts closer. "So you're telling me that I need to ask? Okay…" Guy touches my lips. "Will you kiss me?"

"I don't know if I can."

"Or do I have to kiss you?"

I have no idea what to say, shaking from the slightest touch, denying the desire I have for this strange man who I want, but could never stand to fall in love with and lose. Breaking his gaze and the intensity of the moment, I dip my head.

He sighs. "No problem, I'll keep my lips to myself."

"Until it rains."

"Until it rains and then do I have permission?"

"Maybe."

He gives a small shake of his head. "Bloody Perth summers. Can we go to Melbourne, there's more chance you'll kiss me there?"

I could kiss him. Now. Here. We're seconds away; all that's needed is one of us to take the step. A step to

Guy and back into the deep water.

A taxi appears nearby, and with it the excuse to break this before I throw myself into Guy's arms and lose myself in the fantasy of the handsome prince who rescued me almost three months ago.

"I'll call you tomorrow, Belle," he calls as I head to the waiting car. "And see you next week for the next item!"

CHAPTER TEN

Guy doesn't contact me the next day. Or for several more. This is unusual because we talk at least once every couple of days.

On the second day, I send him a text asking if he's okay and receive no response.

Did I upset him that much? If this is because I wouldn't kiss him, I'm glad I didn't. Guy's looking for somebody whose shoes I can't fill; I'm frightened of becoming emotionally attached to Guy and a kiss or sex would be the first move toward that. What if I'd relented and kissed him, been swept up in the moment, and we'd continued the fantasy and spent the night together?

Three more days and three more texts, nothing. My concern something serious could be wrong with Guy has retreated and is replaced by disappointment. I get the hint.

His rejection pushes confusion and irritation into my days, and I look over my list. Should I plan one without him? But each item I consider feels like a betrayal to my pact with Guy.

After three weeks of trying to contact him with no

response, I take my list from the fridge and push the paper into a kitchen drawer so I don't have to be reminded of him each time I open the fridge door. I will continue the list, with or without him.

****

The opportunity to work on one of the items arises a week later; and I'm certain if it weren't for the list, I'd never consider doing this.

My morning visits to the cafe and Ross have multiplied to include post-work visits too. In a non-stalkerish way, I'm now aware he doesn't work Tuesdays or Monday evenings. I still visit the cafe on those days, in case my growing interest in Ross becomes apparent to the rest of the staff if I miss those days.

Hiding behind my laptop as usual, I pretend I'm working; but instead, research my own articles, ready for the day I crazily believe I'll be allowed to publish one in *Belle de Jour*. The chair opposite me scrapes and somebody sits. I look up and straight into a pair of beautiful, brown eyes, with eyelashes I couldn't achieve without ten layers of mascara.

"Is it okay if I sit here?" Ross asks. He might have the chocolate eyes, but I'm the one melting here; I go from not being interested in men, to a desire for two in the space of a month.

"Sure."

Ross sets his coffee cup on the table in front of him, slender fingers curled around. He wears the usual black work shirt with the cafe logo on and his dark hair contrasts his pale skin. I guess days in a coffee shop don't allow for much time in the sun, or he could be a sensible skin cancer avoiding person.

But those eyes.

"Working?" he asks and sips his drink, ironically the smell of chocolate drifts to me.

"Yes."

"What do you do? You must work near here because of the times you come in, and how you dress." He indicates my blue silk blouse, indicating in the process, he's the kind of man who can control the impulse to stare at women's breasts.

"*Belle de Jour*. Trainee."

"And woman of few words," he says and flashes straight, white teeth to match his other perfection. Jesus, I'm obsessed. And confused. Wasn't I considering cosying up with a surfer a few weeks ago? No, Guy's left the picture. I demonstrate the conversational skills of a three year old by not responding with anything at all.

Bucket list.

Do it.

Ross sat here, didn't he? That's halfway.

"Did you want to meet up some time?" I blurt.

I cringe at the surprise in Ross's otherwise cool expression. Crap, he'll say no and I can't even pretend I'm drunk.

"Well, you saved me asking," he replies.

"Did I?" I shake my head. "God, I sound like an idiot."

"You're sweet."

"Sweet?" I wrinkle my nose.

"Don't forget, I see you come in here every day. I'm a people watcher, which is why I love my job. I can tell a lot about how people behave when they're in here. You, Phe, are sweet to people. The time you paid for the guy's coffee who was a dollar short. Helping mums with prams out of the door when I know you're running late? And impossibly polite. Sweet."

"Oh. Right." The compliment doesn't feel like one to me, but if he likes sweet girls, I'll take it.

"Where were you planning to take me?" he asks.

"I hadn't got that far."

"Good thing I had. Are you busy after work

tonight?"

"Yes. No. I mean, crap."

The half-smile tipping his mouth at one corner suggests he's used to girls blabbering around him. I'm not used to blabbering around men. "Yes or no?"

"Today's Monday."

"Sure is. Restaurant? Bar? Movies? All?"

"Um." My mind cycles through the options. Movies, no chance to talk; what if he only likes car chases and gunfights. Pub, I'll only get drunk. Restaurant, I'm fussy; what if he takes me to somewhere I don't like?

"A meal?" I suggest.

"Restaurant it is then. Your choice."

"Yes."

"Which is?"

"Pardon?"

"Your choice."

"Oh. Um." Maybe the movies would have been the best choice because the chances of us having a conversation seem slim if this continues. "There're a few nice places in Subi."

"Okay, cool. Want me to pick you up?"

"I'm fine. I'll text you with my choice later."

Ross's eyes shine. He pulls my receipt from the edge of the coffee cup and scrawls a phone number on. "Sounds good." Then he stands and inclines his head to the door. "I'd best prepare for my date. Eight?"

I nod, hanging onto the word 'date' as I watch his tall figure leave the cafe, taking my breath with him.

As I finish my coffee, my mind wanders back to the few times I met Guy. Weird, we grew closer to each other; and even though I fought against the attraction I have to him, I didn't think my rejection would end things between us so readily. Tangling with Guy made no sense, and now I'm doubly pleased I didn't kiss him. Ross would be a much more suitable, normal date.

The Same Deep Water

****

I dump the short dress onto the growing pile of clothes on my bed. Half a dozen changes and I'm no closer to choosing. White capri pants and fitted pink top. No. Three variations of summer dress. No. Bugger it. I pull on black skinny jeans and a loose fitting white top that scoops low against my neck. The tattoos catch my eye in the bathroom mirror as I put lipstick on. They still take me by surprise when I see the birds; but I love them, and I'm now considering my next tattoo.

Scouting around the lounge for my low-heeled boots, my phone beeps and my stomach lurches. What if Ross is cancelling? I grab the phone from the table.

<Phe :) How's things?>

Guy. After three weeks of ignoring me, he sends a text as if we only spoke yesterday?

<Okay thanks>

I place the phone down and it beeps again <I have my bucket list item>

<I'm busy. I'll text later>

<Busy?>

<Going out>

This time I switch off the phone and shove it in my bag. Guy contacted me; but after ignoring me for weeks, I'm not dropping everything for him.

I can't switch my phone off. What if Ross calls? I click the on button and within a minute, the phone beeps again.

<Can we meet?>

<I'll text later>

<Is this because I haven't been in touch? I was sick>

Right, sick for three weeks. On the verge of texting those words back, I pause. I bet he doesn't mean flu.

<Are you okay now?>

<Just got home. Bored. Can we meet?>

81

<I said I'm going out>

<Oh. Maybe later?>

<For the evening. Meeting someone.>

<Belle... Did you find a Prince Charming?>

I glance at the clock on the DVD player. 7.00pm. <I'm running late>

<No problem. Wish I could see you and not kiss you again>

Guy has never asked to see me. Not in such strong terms. How sick is he?

<Are you alright?>

<No>

I chew my lip, torn over what to do. He helped me when I needed, and in a roundabout way is asking for my help too.

But I want to see Ross. He's not my Prince Charming, but he's the object of lustful fantasies; the man who could distract me from my pull toward a dying man I also fantasise about, but who I'm certain will break my heart.

<Where do you want to meet?> I text.

<You sure?>

<Yes>

<Usual?>

Do I call Ross or text him? Am I blowing my only chance here?

One awkward conversation with Ross later, I head to the cafe where I often meet Guy.

Guy sits in his usual spot, and looks around as I approach. I pull up a chair and sit too. He's pale, eyes less bright than usual, and wearing a smart shirt and jeans. His hair is different, buzz cut around the back and sides, shorter on top

"Image change?" I ask.

"My hair was annoying me. Thanks for coming."

"That's okay. Sounds like you need someone to talk to. You helped me when I needed it." I move to take his hand, but stop myself.

"Ah, but I only spoke to you when you needed because you were on my list." He smiles weakly.

"Way to make a girl feel special."

He smirks, but doesn't apologise.

"Why were you really there that night?" I ask in a low voice. "Was that true about the flowers?"

Guy rubs his lips together and watches me. "Omnia causa fiunt."

"What does that mean?"

"Look it up." He picks up his cup. "Tell me about your Prince Charming."

I blink at his subject change. "I don't have one."

"So you weren't going on a date?"

"I was, but it was the first."

"Oh. Shit. Sorry I spoilt things for you."

"It's fine, we've re-arranged. Ticked an item off my list though, I asked him."

I expect Guy to laugh in agreement; but instead, he focuses on the cup in his hands. "Good. I hope he's a nice guy."

"I came here to talk about you, not me."

Guy drains his coffee. "Yeah. Let me buy these."

This Guy's manner is different to usual. He hovers back from the counter, letting others in front of him, hands in pockets. The confidence is missing. He avoids my eyes when he returns and sits and pushes the cup to me.

"You always drink the same, which is why I never asked," he says.

"I wasn't going to say anything. It's fine."

Guy takes his time opening a sachet of sugar and tipping the contents into his cup. Do I ask him? Wait for him to say?

"You said you'd been sick. Are you okay now?"

"Yeah. Had to go to hospital for a couple of weeks."

"Oh. That's not good. Are you...?"

He continues to focus on stirring his coffee. "I'm alright. A weekly check-up is all I need for now."

I relax. "You still have time, don't you? To do what you want."

Guy looks up. "Yes. For now."

I can't go on with this friendship unless I understand what's happening. If we have a friendship and Guy needs my support, he needs to let me know what's wrong with him.

"Your illness. Is it something that will stop you physically first? I mean, do you only have a certain amount of time before you can't walk or something?"

"That's blunt."

"I don't know how else to ask. You won't tell me what's wrong with you."

"You never asked again."

"What's wrong with you?"

"I'd rather not say."

I place my hands under the table and he watches. "I don't have something contagious, so don't worry your pretty head about that. Whatever we decide to do together, I won't give this to you. It's all inside me and isn't coming out."

Cancer? Why does he keep avoiding my eyes? He behaves like any other normal person whenever I see him; and I understand this is something he may not want to talk about, but I'm fed up with trying to figure this out. How can this man with his infectious nature who embraces everything life has to offer him be dying? And why won't he tell me?

We drink coffee in silence as dusk sets in. Groups chatter around us, meeting for coffees, and preparing for their own nights out. Several couples sit close together, touching and connecting.

The conversation about our almost kiss obviously isn't happening. I wish I were more clued up on body language; he seems guarded, which makes sense. How bigheaded of me to think he hadn't contacted me because I'd rejected him when the obvious answer was illness.

The way Guy held me when he danced, the feel of his arms around me sticks though, and the desire to have this again was behind my asking Ross on a date. If I could find another man who wants to hold me and kiss me, I don't have to fight my feelings for Guy.

Feelings? Physical attraction that would lead to an emotional attachment I'm unsure I want. One that's happening involuntarily. I now struggle to sit close to Guy without remembering his strength and warmth. I don't hug people; touching anybody is rare and his embrace tapped a hole into the wall against the need for physical contact. Just as he drew me from the edge three months ago, he's pulling me to a stronger bond with the world – a human one.

Bucket list. Partners. Subject change. "So, your list. Which did you come up with to do next?" I ask.

"I want to skydive."

"I've no idea why you would, but okay."

He straightens in his chair, eyes brightening. "Plus, I can take you surfing. We can take a weekend out."

"A weekend where?"

"South. There's a skydiving company down there, great views of the coast from the plane."

"That you intend to jump out of even though the plane's functioning perfectly."

He makes a soft sound of amusement and watches me expectantly.

"Oh. Um." A weekend. Us. "I might be busy."

"You're worried about going away with me?"

"No. Yes. I don't know. After the other night..."

"I promise not to kiss you, even if it rains." He smiles. "Invite your housemate, I know somebody who has a holiday place near Dunsborough. Practically beach front." He pauses. "Lots of bedrooms."

I rub my hands together under the table. Why do I have so many items on my bucket list that include water? "I'm not sure about the surfing just yet."

"Come on, Phe. Best time of year. Plus, you're still several items behind me."

"Aren't there a lot of sharks around that part of the coast?"

"Even better, two birds with one stone. You surf, I swim with sharks." He grins.

I shake my head at him. The challenge to myself to overcome my fear of water could be about to take a step in the right direction.

"This weekend?" I ask.

"The sooner the better, time is of the essence and all that crap." Guy picks at the edge of a napkin, the darkness flickering in his eyes again, before he looks up. "If you're free."

What the hell, why not? "Okay."

We step back from the brink of the subjects we avoid and spend the next hour together. Over a meal, we chat – mostly about what I've been doing in the time apart, our meeting feeling more like a date by the minute.

We easily slip back into the comfort of each other's company until by the end of the evening, I'm aware how relaxed I am around Guy and how much I missed him.

CHAPTER ELEVEN

Six months in Perth and I've never ventured far from the city and suburbs; friends from work often go "Down South" to the Margaret River region at weekends. Focused on my everyday routine in an attempt to stay grounded, taking impromptu breaks away hasn't been on my agenda.

Guy picks me up in a Jeep this time and I query how many cars he has. He tells me four, with a teasing grin, but I'm not entirely sure he's joking. A worn surfboard is strapped to the roof rack, which I avoid looking at – or thinking about throwing myself to the mercy of the waves.

The drive takes less than three hours, the highway heading through the urban sprawl of Perth until the buildings thin to brown bush bordering the straight roads instead.

Guy looks tired again today, not unwell, but shadowed eyes as if he isn't sleeping. He's back to the quirky-humoured Guy I usually spend time with; but after our meeting the other day, I'm more aware that his smile hides secrets.

"Are you feeling okay at the moment?" I ask.

"I'm all good, Ophelia."

"Don't call me that," I snap back. "Phe."

"I think Ophelia's a great name."

"I don't. Don't use it."

Guy purses his lips and keeps driving. "Why?"

"Because I don't like her story."

"Yours or hers?"

I look out of the window, at the world flying past the window, blurred and monotonous. "Both."

"Were you ever called Ophelia?"

"Drop it."

"Phe is a strange abbreviation, though."

"Lia." I swallow. "I was Lia."

"And why aren't you –"

"Shut up!" The idea of opening the car door and jumping out launches into my mind, as my brain's illogical misfiring suggests I climb out of a moving car to escape a threat that doesn't exist.

Guy glances from the road to me, unable to hide the surprise in his eyes. "I notice you're working on the assertive thing. Good to see."

"Like I said before, you don't know me well. Certain things piss me off. Like this." I don't want tension to start our weekend. I intend to relax and have fun instead of the structured routine, which I apply to my life at weekends too.

"Under that carefully constructed exterior you're a passionate girl then?"

I side glance him and his eyes are on the road, mouth quirked into a smile at one corner.

"I guess we both have stories that are painful."

Guy taps the steering wheel. "I won't ask you yours, if you don't ask me mine."

"Okay." But it's not. Each time I move closer to Guy, I hit a barrier. Originally, I thought the barriers between us were all mine, but his become more visible each time. I run through what he's told me about himself and I know little: he's sick, he's wealthy, likes the outdoors, and sometimes he paints. What about his family? He mentioned a sister but that's all. Where are they? Why is he living alone?

A weekend with Guy and I'm going to find some answers.

The sound of his eclectic mix of tracks on the car stereo travels with us for the next hour, conversation ceasing. I'm not the only one holding someone at arm's length. Is Guy's confusion over what we are or could become as great as mine?

Guy's friends' house is set back from the beach, on a gentle hill, overlooking the Indian Ocean. The modern building is at odds with the nature around, the angular lines giving the building the feel of an office block. The property has been designed to maximise the views with a large balcony wrapped around the upper floor. Several similar houses surround, with older shack-like properties nestling between. The price of beachfront land around here doesn't tempt everybody to sell.

The beach across the narrow road fills the house too – via colourful blue and yellow furnishings and coastal pictures on the white walls. Art made from shells and driftwood and signs painted "to the beach" adorn the wicker furniture creating a classic holiday-by-the sea ambience. I walk to the floor to ceiling window at the front of the house and look down at the clear, flat ocean. The early afternoon sun enhances the the picture postcard blue of the water.

"This place is amazing," I say. "So quiet and beautiful."

"This is a great place to come for an escape."

The tension from the journey ebbs; holding onto stress would be impossible in an environment like this.

"What time are your friends arriving?" Guy asks as he joins me.

"Late afternoon. Jen's working."

"Time for a surf lesson then," he says.

I clench my jaw and fix my eyes on the water. "Not yet. I'm tired."

"A walk on the beach then?"

My bag rests next to Guy's feet where he's dropped it, and I pick up the full rucksack. "I'll unpack first."

"Master suite upstairs and three back there." He points to a door at the opposite end of the open plan room and takes my bag. "You can have upstairs."

I follow him up the narrow stairs. "Are you sure? Shouldn't we let Jen and Cam have the room? They're the couple."

"Nope. You're the important guest and this one has the en suite and views."

The upstairs bedroom floods with light through double-glass doors leading to the balcony. I sit on the edge of the huge bed. The luxury of the bedding and the modern, sleek bathroom I can see through a half-open door put me in mind of a hotel.

"Wow."

Guy crosses the room and slides open the balcony's doors. At home, this would let in traffic sounds, but here there's nothing but the call of the magpies in the trees below. "Pretty special, hey?"

"Absolutely." Eager for a clear view, I stand with him. The gum trees border the opposite road and directly behind them a pathway leads through brown scrub toward the white sandy beach. The balcony's position offers panoramic views of Geographe Bay, the pristine blue waters calm. A dream location for any beach lover.

"You like?"

I nod, soaking in the peace of the environment. The sky is cloudless, the view perfect.

"Are you sure?" He taps his teeth. "You don't look sure and you've been quiet on the journey. Would you rather be here with Prince Charming?"

I look at him in surprise. "No, and don't call him

that. I hardly know Ross, so no."

I cancelled our re-arranged date and I know why.

I'm fighting my attraction to Guy hard, and failing.

The undercurrents are there, a tide pulling us back and forth. Close together in an empty house, next to a large bed and the unsaid between us grows louder. The hair on my arms prickles at his proximity, close enough to catch his subtle scent reminding me of our dance. At the masquerade ball, I screwed things up by denying I wanted him to kiss me, because logic stepped in and put a hand out to stop me.

I look past him. "Great view from here too."

"Amazing views at sunset," he replies in a low voice. "Do you?"

"Do I what?"

"Wish you were here with somebody else?"

"I couldn't possibly be. Nobody else I know would be stupid enough to jump out of a functional aeroplane."

He breaks his serious face with one of his dimpled smiles. "I can't wait! Here, unpack. We can have a beach walk."

Guy thrusts my bag at me, edges past, and disappears downstairs. Dazed, I stare out at the ocean again. Why do I feel as if he's testing me?

****

Jen stacks the plates from the large jarrah dining table, and I gather the serving bowls and cutlery. As we head into the kitchen, she nudges me hard in the ribs and I stumble.

"Phe! You kept quiet about him!" she hisses. "What's going on?"

"What do you mean?"

Arching a brow, Jen sets the plates on the marble

counter next to the sink. "When you said we were spending the weekend at a friend's house, I thought you meant a girl from work! How long have you been with him? Why didn't you tell me?"

"He *is* a friend." I pull open the dishwasher drawer and drop cutlery into the basket. For now. By the end of the weekend, I'm not so sure.

"You think?" She cranes her neck to look through the kitchen door behind. "How do you keep your hands off him?"

Good question and one with a complicated answer. "This is one of those situations where I don't want to lose his friendship."

"How do you know you will? You seem very in tune together. Besides, more than a friendship could lead to some exciting times." Jen nudges me again and I elbow her back.

"Behave, Jen!"

"Just saying. He's the whole package – good-looking guy, smoking hot body, and sense of humour. He seems smart too."

"He is."

"So what's the problem? He's into you; that's obvious."

I turn away and focus on the dishwasher again. Is it? "Things might not work out. He's... leaving soon."

"So? Have some fun before he goes! Surely, you're not looking for somebody to settle down with?"

"Not at all." But a broken-heart could send me spiralling in a direction I don't want.

She glances at the door. "If I wasn't with Cam, I'd push you out of the way! Far out, Phe, grab some while you can! Don't you just want to lick him inch by inch? Those abs..."

I chew the inside of my lip rather than follow this line of conversation. Yes, I do. And more. She and Cam arrived a little after seven and she'd poured her first generous glass of red wine within minutes. I've lost count of the number she's had.

Earlier, Guy took me to a local produce market where we selected fresh fish and farm-fresh vegetables, before heading to a bottle shop where Guy selected his favourite local wine. The Margaret River region is filled with wineries so the selection took some time. The date-like air doesn't escape me; but instead of causing tension, I relax into the holiday atmosphere.

Later we cooked the meal together while we waited for Cam and Jen's arrival, Guy expertly preparing the fish while I took the backseat and prepared the vegetables. Admittedly, I was already a couple of glasses of a nice, local sav blanc ahead of Jen when they arrived. Vegetables don't take long to prepare and I spent time resting against the kitchen bench watching Guy, blindingly aware how happy and relaxed I am around him. What happens next?

Jen points behind me. "Grab the vodka. I've had enough of wine."

"Jen..."

She sticks her bottom lip out. "Hey, I'm on holiday!" She reaches past and grabs the bottle.

I follow Jen back out of the kitchen. Guy sits at the table, leaning back in his chair with one leg crossed over the other, happy, and laughing at something with Cam as they drink their bottled beers. Ordinary, everyday blokes in ordinary, everyday lives. Why did Guy suggest this? To pull us from our world of bucket lists and into a reality that we're on the edge of? Another couple, living in the moment, but planning a future.

What have I done? Inviting Jen and Cam here too was supposed to be a sign to Guy this wasn't a trip about 'us', but 'Guy and Phe'. Now I've created the illusion of two couples holidaying together.

"Sofas! Now! Drinking games," says Jen, waving the vodka and shot glasses in their direction.

I expect Guy to laugh and join in, but his smile freezes.

"I'm not sure..." I start.

"Live life while you're still young!" she interrupts, scowling at me.

"Guy's jumping out of a plane tomorrow, he might not want to be hungover," I reply, glancing at Guy.

Cam laughs. "All the more reason to. If everything goes wrong, he could have a live fast, die young moment!" He throws a cork from the table at Guy to attract his attention. "How fast do you fall?"

Guy picks at the label on his bottle. "Fast. I fall really fast."

As he says the words, Guy looks at me. His deep blue eyes are unfathomable; but his words concern me. I fight against reaching out to touch his hand. As each minute passes, I question the wisdom of allowing my two worlds to collide.

Giving in to Jen's badgering, I settle on the large yellow sofa and Guy sits on the floor near my feet. Jen and Cam cuddle up on the opposite blue sofa, Jen's legs tucked under her. We chat between shots, or Jen burbles. Guy says little. Half an hour and a bottle of vodka later, the world swims. Jen's enthusiasm for drinking games borders on peer pressure.

"I don't drink much usually," says Guy, resting his head on the sofa. "I should stop." His cheek touches my legs as he leans back and looks up at me. "So, excuse me if I say weird shit."

"Ooh! That gives me a good idea!" enthuses Jen. "Truth or dare!"

Cam groans. "Jen, we're not thirteen!"

"It'll be fun! I want to find out more about the mysterious Guy." She giggles and places the empty vodka bottle on the rug between the two sofas. "He doesn't talk about himself, have you noticed?"

"I'm not that interesting," he replies stiffly.

"What do you do?" she asks.

"Nothing."

"For a job, I mean."

"Nothing. I'm taking time out. Living fast, dying young."

In her drunken state, Jen misses the sarcasm. "Nice if you can afford to."

Guy shuffles forward. "Spin the bottle?"

"Oh! Yeah! Game!"

Nicely fielded, Guy.

Fortunately, the bottle stops at Jen, which I swear is what she wanted. "Truth!" She looks to Cam. "You ask!"

Cam smiles slyly at Jen and leans so his face is near hers. "Have you ever kissed a girl?"

"Of course! Hasn't everybody?" She places a quick kiss on his lips then throws her hands up. "That wasn't very interesting."

The bottle spins again and points at me. "My turn!" calls Jen.

I cringe. I hope this isn't going where I think. Dare could mean kissing her. "Truth."

"What's one thing nobody in this room knows about you?" she asks.

The obvious springs to mind, the accident, the deaths. The night with Guy on the rocks at least doesn't factor in because he knows. I can't give a voice to the memories of my family and choose a safer option. "I grew up living with my grandparents."

"Really? I wondered why you never spoke about your parents. Is the story bad about them? What happened? Did they die?" slurs Jen.

Cam puts his hand over her mouth. "She's a heartless drunk. Jen, be quiet."

"Phe mentioned them!"

"They're dead, yes," I say and push the bottle which stops, pointing at me again.

"Hey! No fair! Two goes! Or are you gonna ask yourself a question?" replies Jen.

Cam looks at me in embarrassed shock at his girlfriend's dismissive behaviour; and to my surprise, Guy curls his hand around mine.

"Did you hear what she said?" Guy asks Jen.

"When?"

Cam takes the glass from her hands. "Memory blanks are supposed to come later not within minutes!"

"Oh. Right. I'm sorry about your parents."

"It's fine." I rub my face. "Why am I doing this?"

"Was that your question?"

"Yeah."

Jen continues her obliviousness to the growing atmosphere in the room. "I'll go again." The vodka bottle whirls into a blur on the shaggy teal rug, and rests somewhere between Guy and Cam. "Closer to Guy!"

Guy's silence in the last few minutes worries me, tension rolling from him. From my position, I can't see his expression and wish I could. "Dare," he says in a low voice.

A slow smile crosses Jen's face. "I was hoping you'd say that. Kiss Phe."

"Truth," he throws back.

Heat crosses my face, at the embarrassment from Jen's words and his refusal. This is bad. Really bad. And becoming worse by the minute.

"Hmm. Let me think," she says.

Cam leans over and whispers in Jen's ear. Her expression of concentration switches to eagerness. "Tell me, mysterious Guy, what's the worst thing you've done in your life?"

My heart thumps with every second he doesn't reply, Jen poking the wasps nest of the secrets he keeps.

"There's quite a choice," he replies. "How bad?"

"How bad? Ohmigod. Have you killed somebody?" She collapses in another fit of giggles, her white blonde hair falling across her face.

I swallow and stand. "I don't think this game is working, Jen. I should go to bed."

Guy looks up at me from the floor, eyes glittering. "She asked. I'll tell her."

"I don't want to know," I whisper.

I glare at Jen who's now sitting forward, elbows on her knees and hands beneath her chin, expectantly.

Guy stands and looks straight at Jen. "I killed my mother."

Guy's words echo inside my drunk brain and I shake my head in case I misheard. Guy shoves his hands in his jeans pockets and continues to regard Jen. Her giggling stops and she straightens. "What?"

"He's taking the piss," remarks Cam. "You're pushing people into doing and saying things they don't want."

Guy did say the words. The world lurches. No, Cam's right, he's lying to shut Jen up.

"We're playing truth or dare!" mutters Jen. "That's the whole point of the game!"

Is he? Did he? "Guy?"

"It's true," he says, not looking at me.

"Sure it is! That's why you're walking the streets and not locked up!" says Jen sarcastically.

"You only wanted an answer, not an explanation. And I'm not playing your stupid, fucking game anymore!" Guy grabs his half-empty beer from the table and storms barefoot out of the house, the front door slamming behind him.

We stare after him, and nobody speaks for a while.

"Whoa. Reckon he did?" Jen rests her head on the sofa. "Psycho."

I hesitate, looking in the direction of the door. Do I follow him? As I step towards the front door, Cam sits up. "You're not going after him are you?"

"Yes."

"What? He told us he killed somebody and you're going to follow him into the dark?"

"I'm not scared of him and I don't believe him."

"Ohmigod! What if now he's told us, Guy's gonna kill us too!" shrieks Jen.

"Jen, you're wasted. Don't be fucking stupid," Cam says, and then looks to me. "Are you sure? Normal people don't say shit like that."

"Guy's not normal people and neither am I." I slip my feet into my strappy sandals and walk into the night.

CHAPTER TWELVE

A streetlight a few hundred metres away doesn't offer much illumination, but the large moon picks out a figure striding through the scrub toward the beach. I hurry across the empty road to catch up.

"Guy!" He either doesn't hear or ignores me. I blink as I step from the lit road to the beach, adjusting my eyes until I see his figure again. "Guy!"

The sand fills my sandals and slows me down as I jog closer to him. I call his name once more, louder and he halts. He can't pretend he doesn't hear me in the silence of the early hours.

Guy turns, the moonlight picking out his drawn features. "Why have you followed me?"

"Because I'm worried about you."

"Huh."

The gap between us is small, but feels like a chasm I'm unsure I can cross. Why did he say what he did? This man in the moonlit shadows isn't the Guy I know. He swears under his breath and sits.

When Guy doesn't speak, I join him on the sand; and for a few moments, we stare at the ocean.

"I should've taken the dare and kissed you," he

says, "But she pissed me off."

"You certainly shut her up."

Guy digs his fingers into the sand next to him. "It was the truth," he says. "I did kill my mother."

I control the gasp of breath threatening to escape. "Then why aren't you..."

"In prison? She died a long time ago. I was a kid."

The waves lap the shore, the darkened water close to my feet and I wriggle back, not wanting water to touch me. Guy spoke about this tonight for a reason, he didn't need to; he had a choice. "Do you want to tell me what happened?"

"She died giving birth to me. I killed her," he says, voice void of emotion.

"Guy..." I place a hand on his arm. "No, you didn't. That's tragic but you can't think like that." He doesn't move or respond. "I'm sure you've been told this a thousand times."

Guy takes my hand and pushes it away. "I hurt people, Phe. I kill people. I came into this world by taking a life. All my life, people I become close to suffer. I'm a curse. I deserve to die."

The evening breeze lifts the hairs on the back of my neck. Guy won't look at me and his words are slurred around the edges; dredged from his depths I had no idea about.

"Don't say things like that! I don't believe you're a bad person."

"You don't know me, Phe."

"Because you hide yourself."

"I guess I'm not hidden anymore then, am I?"

I take his hand again. "I want to know what kind of man you are beneath the surface, because I think he's a good man."

"Things are complicated." He curls his cool fingers around mine, and squeezes. "I feel cursed."

Guy shifts closer, our legs touching. Would a

normal person shy away from him? At this moment, I want his closeness more than ever, to show him I don't agree. That I care. The dark water nearby quietly laps the shore, hardly audible beneath Guy's stressed breathing

"Since you know something about me, can I ask you something?" he asks.

"What?"

"You said your parents were dead. What happened?"

An exchange of secrets, slipping through a crack in the barrier between the part of Guy that recognises part of Phe, and wants to take hold. I take my hand away and wrap my arms around my knees.

"Remember I told you their death was an accident? It wasn't."

"Oh."

I heave a breath. "I got out."

"Out of where?"

"I can't talk about this, Guy, the nightmares will start again."

"I understand all about nightmares."

"I understand about feeling cursed," I whisper back.

Guy touches my cheek and I tremble, against the cool breeze on the beach, the fear dug up, and the need for Guy to take hold of me. Guy looks the same as at the cafe last Monday – tired and defeated – and my heart hurts for him. "I want to explain so much, but I can't. I don't know how to."

"You don't need to until you're ready."

Guy wraps an arm around my shoulders and I rest my head against his hard chest. "Why do you trust me?" he asks.

"Shouldn't I trust you?"

"I just told you I hurt everybody who's close to me."

"How can you say that after what you did for

me?"

His lack of response worries me and I move to look at him. Guy takes my hand and traces the lines on my palm. "When I saw you in the dark, I had to fight against running over and dragging you away from the edge. I wanted to hold you, to absorb your suffering. I'm sick of hurting people. I thought taking away your pain might absolve me somehow."

"I don't believe you hurt people, Guy."

"I don't hurt people deliberately. It just happens." He takes a deep breath and looks at me. "Since the moment I saw you on the edge, I've wanted us, but I'm scared. I don't want anything to happen to you."

I touch his face. "You've already helped me so much. That first night and in the days after."

Guy looks at my hands. "I messaged you every evening so that every time you closed your eyes to sleep you would know somebody out there cared."

Guy's words choke me; the carefully hidden man revealing the fractured edges of his soul and the depth of his heart. "Being with you is transforming my world, and I don't think the list is the only reason, is it?"

"What if I do hurt you?"

"Then I'll cope."

"Will you?"

I understand his need to pull me from the edge. I share the hatred that another person could hurt in the same way. All this time and I failed to notice, too busy struggling against the dark tide threatening to pull me under. Guy is swimming the same deep water as me.

"Yes. I can't hide from the world and deny the good for fear of the bad. You live in the moment and I should too," I tell him.

Guy laughs softly and touches my cheek. "Living dangerously, Phe. You'll be jumping out of planes next."

I shake my head. "Maybe I'll pass on living in that particular moment."

"So what happens?" he asks, cupping my cheek in his hands.

"I don't want to wait until it rains." I shift closer to him, willing him to embrace me.

"You're crazy."

"We already know that."

Exhaling, Guy curls his hand into my hair, and then rests his forehead against mine, warm breath heating my face. "This pulls us into something different. I'm not sure."

"Kiss me, even if only once." I move my head so our lips touch the buzz of connection immediate.

"If I kiss you it will be more than once."

"Good." I turn my face and meet his mouth curling a hand around his neck to pull him closer. Guy places one hand in the sand, circles his other arm around my waist, and he kisses me. The warm pressure of his mouth moves from tentative to firmer as I push my lips against his, eagerly responding and pressing myself into him. Mouth harder against mine, Guy parts my lips, exploring as I push my tongue against his.

We kiss for what feels like forever, a single moment frozen in time, not moving or closing the rest of the space between us. I crave Guy's hands on my skin, to slide my hands against his too, but this should stay as a kiss.

Guy pulls away slowly, as if he doesn't want to take his lips from mine, and releases my waist. We could kiss again, our lips close enough that they still feel connected, and I'm tempted. I move my head back; but in the dim, I can barely make out Guy's expression.

"There's something strange about us," he says.

I laugh. "You reckon?"

"No, about us. Together. Do you think we cancel each other out?"

"What do you mean?"

"Life and death."

"Don't talk about death when I just kissed you, Guy. That was to distract you."

"Not because you wanted to kiss me?"

"That too."

Guy holds my face with both hands and kisses me softly again. "Being with you changed my world, Phe. I'm not sure I can ever go back to my old one."

"The world's a brighter place with you in, that's for sure." I take his hand and squeeze. "I don't want to talk about the bad or the past."

Guy tucks a strand of hair behind my ear. "I don't want to stay here. Let's go back to the house and hope your stupid friend has passed out drunk."

I walk with Guy back to the house, a line crossed. We could be any couple giving in to our attraction, taking a tentative step in the direction we both want to go. But we're not.

Light from the half-open front door shines onto the pathway and we step inside to an empty lounge room. Empty bottles and glasses remain strewn around the room, but Jen and Cam are gone. A subdued Guy sits on the sofa and rubs sand from his feet.

I look up as I hear a noise from the kitchen. Cam hesitates in the doorway with two large glasses of water, and a rueful smile.

"Hey," he says.

"Hey," I reply.

Guy says nothing.

I'm relieved when Cam ends the conversation at an exchanged greeting and heads to the back of the house with his drinks. Guy watches, and back in the light I can see more clearly how drunk he is. The fresh air didn't do much for my sobriety either, nor does the light-headed feeling from Guy's kiss.

His mouth curves into a smile and he flops against the back of the sofa. "Do you think they believed me, about my mother?"

I sit next to him. "Probably not."

"She's a bit obnoxious, your mate." He drags a hand down his face. "Sorry, she's your friend, but she's rude."

"Jen's always like that when she's drunk."

He smooths hair from my face and cups my cheek. "Like I said, should've just kissed you if I knew you were going to anyway."

Before I can respond, Guy's lips find mine again and he draws me back from the craziness of the evening into the calm of his embrace. His kiss is slow, holding my head instead of moving to touch my skin. Pausing, he buries his face in my neck, exhales heavily, and squeezes me.

I stroke his hair. "Are you alright?"

"Drunk. Wishing I'd kept my mouth shut."

I hold him and fight the arousal triggered by his kiss. Guy's rough cheek scrapes against my skin as he places his lips on my collarbone. We remain in silence and the drunken warmth of our embrace coupled with Guy's rhythmic breathing conspires against me. I begin to nod off as Guy's body becomes heavier against mine.

"I can't fall asleep here," I murmur.

Stretching and shaking his head to wake himself, Guy studies me as we reach the moment things could shift further. "You going to bed?"

"I was going to go, yes. Will you be okay?"

"Me? Yeah." He places his lips on my forehead. "I'd like to join you, but I don't think that's a good idea."

My breath catches, the alcohol-numbed morals suggesting I could ask him to. "Right."

Guy stands and tugs me to my feet. "If you weren't as drunk as me, I'd be suggesting all kinds of things to you."

"So when we're sober, what then?"

"Then, I will have lots of suggestions," he says in a low voice.

When we part, I lie in bed and mull the last few hours over in my head. Fate is a strange creature, drawing together lost souls then stepping back to watch what happens. What worries me is how kissing Guy felt right and how natural being in his company feels.

How can this end well?

CHAPTER THIRTEEN

#5 Go Skydiving

Breakfast holds tension. A hungover Jen nurses a steaming cup of coffee when I arrive downstairs, and Guy is in the kitchen buttering toast. Without speaking to Jen, I head into the kitchen to Guy.

"How are you?" I ask. "Ready for today?"

He licks butter from his fingers. "Yep. It's not too late to join me, you know."

"I don't think so! Your bucket list, not mine."

"You're staying to watch then?"

"That's why I came here this weekend."

"Right." He takes a bite of toast. "Your friends are leaving. I thought you might want to go with them too."

My stomach lurches. He hasn't tried to touch or kiss me since I walked into the room; this was a mistake to him. "Oh. Do you want me to?"

"No, Phe. I don't want you to."

As I busy myself making a cup of tea, Guy remains behind me, and I feel his proximity as if we were touching. "Were you very drunk last night?" he asks.

"Fairly. I think we all were."

"Did you mean to kiss me?"

I turn in surprise. "No, Guy, I tripped and my lips met yours. Why? Didn't you want to?"

"Last night was a mess," he says. "I didn't want you to know those things about me."

"Well, I do now. And so do they." I indicate Jen who now has her head on the table, hair splayed around her. "Are you going to explain?"

"Nah. I'll let her think I'm a fugitive on the run for the murder of his mother."

I look away. We can't go back to this. Not murder. I carry the guilt of the day I survived the murder of my mum and brother. I understand his need to tie the past inside, but I also know how this knots around your soul and devours.

"Good morning, Jen." Guy sits opposite her at the table. He wasn't joking about pretending nothing happened. She shifts and says something I don't hear.

"No worries. We all said some things we didn't want to." He munches on his toast.

An awkward looking, pale Jen joins me in the kitchen. I don't often see her without make-up, her naked lips and unpainted eyes soften her features, and she looks years younger than her twenty-four. "We're leaving this morning."

"Guy told me you were."

"Be careful, Phe," she says in a low voice. "I don't know if I trust him."

"I do." I dump the teabag in the bin and pour milk into my cup. "I trust him more than anybody."

Jen's brows shoot up. "Then I think you're asking for trouble."

"Yesterday you were all for matchmaking us."

"Oh, God, don't start a relationship with him." She groans at my small smile. "Phe, no. Did you...?"

"No, but you did. Noisily." Jen wrinkles her nose in response and I sidestep her. "Last night opened my eyes to a few things."

"I hope you know what you're doing."

I look behind her to Guy, who turns his head as if aware of my scrutiny and meets my eyes. I always felt as if Guy saw more of me than anybody else, and now the remaining veil between us is slipping. For the first time in a long time, I know what I want and I'm doing it.

****

The plane drones overhead and I sit on the white sand, shielding my eyes against the sun as I watch. The lucky skydivers experience amazing views of the Bay, though to me the flight would feel like that of a condemned woman. I wouldn't make it out of the plane unless someone physically pushed me or dragged me screaming through the air.

Guy's preparations for the jump took some time and when he handed over his medical and waiver form, it occurred to me he may have lied. Again, I sweep a look at his fit and healthy figure, trying to figure out what's wrong with him. All day I've been hyperaware of his proximity, aching for him. Now I've let somebody through, my body craves more.

I'm also aware I need to hear more secrets from him before I allow myself to fall any further, but that involves giving up more of mine.

A man with two small children joins me on the beach where we wait for the plane to circle back. The little blond-haired boy and girl chase each other between the water and the beach, while the man stands next to me, arms crossed.

"They don't understand why their mum wants to jump out of a plane," he says.

I nod. "I don't understand why anybody would."

"She's doing this for charity, but what if she hurts herself?" He indicates his children. "Or worse."

"I'm sure she's very safe," I say. The concern on

the middle-aged man's face is clear. I never thought to worry about Guy injuring himself.

"I saw you with your boyfriend. Why aren't you jumping too?" he asks.

"I'm not into extreme sports." I laugh. "I'm not into extreme anything."

"Sensible." The little boy tugs at his sleeve, asking for a drink and the man delves into his black rucksack.

Sensible.

That's the problem. I thought sensible would control my world and stop tragedy touching my life again but that already failed once. Sensible numbs. Sensible leaves nothing to drive me on, to live a life I can. But can I go to extremes?

"There she is!" cries the little girl.

Two joined figures, as small as a bird in the sky, fall through the air and my heart lurches into my mouth as I watch. Who jumps first? Is this Guy?

The parachute catches the free-falling pair, yanking them upwards until their descent resumes, slower. This is me and Guy, free falling together until something saves us and slows down the plummet to death.

For one of us at least.

Tears prick my eyes, not because I know I'll lose Guy, but because a man so full of life can have his snatched away when people who barely live are wasting theirs.

Further, along the beach, the skydiver and instructor hit the ground, and then run along the beach. The suited figure is too tall to be the small woman who hugged her children goodbye and whose husband refused to kiss her. The person could be one of the two Dutch backpackers, a couple locked in their excitement before they headed to the waiting plane; but as he approaches, I know this is Guy. A man on the beach helps him out of the parachute and Guy's excitement is reflected in his body language, arms gesturing wildly as he paces from foot to foot.

Guy charges across the sand toward me, invigorated, red cheeks and shining eyes. He sweeps me off my feet. I catch his shoulders in surprise and look down at him. He kisses me hard on the mouth and laughs breathlessly.

"You need to do that! It's fucking awesome!" Guy spins me around, the world out of control, as I lock my arms around his neck. "That is the second most amazing thing I've done in my life!"

"Second? You've led a crazy life if that's not the first! What tops that?"

He sets me down and cups my face in his cold hands. "Kissing you last night."

The intensity is back; his words would sound trite, but are spoken with sincerity. I touch his cheek with a small smile. "Correction, a boring life, if that's number one."

"Don't underestimate yourself and the effect you have on people. You sure as hell have an effect on me." He grabs my ass in both hands and squeezes.

Embarrassed, I glance around at the man and his children; but fortunately, they're looking the other way. "I still can't believe you jumped out of a plane! That's mad!"

"I think everybody should try skydiving!"

Pulled into Guy's enthusiasm, I wrap my arms around his neck and kiss him. His face is damp, heart thundering against my chest as we embrace. He breaks away and lifts me from the sand again, spinning us around until the world blurs into streaks of colour. Dizzy and breathless, I rest my head on Guy's and hold on. We're anchored in our blurred world, out of time and place, and for the first time in my life holding onto somebody else feels right.

****

I wait by the Jeep for Guy to return from changing. The dark grip of last night's weirdness was blown away by his jump and his brand of happiness is infectious, wrapping around and squeezing life into me. If doing something as challenging as Guy did can bring someone to life in this way, I should conquer my fear and take the step into my challenges.

Guy greets me with a kiss when he arrives at the car and my head spins again at the easy shift from friends to couple. "Right. Back to the house for a shower then surfing lesson number one for you!"

"I was waiting to see if you felt up to teaching me, thought you might be tired after your morning."

He draws his brows together in mock sternness. "Ophelia. You're trying to avoid this, aren't you? I thought we agreed."

"I didn't exactly agree." I offer him a sweet smile. "I'd rather not. Besides, look no waves."

"Not here but I know where there are plenty of awesome surfing spots." Guy drops his scrutiny from my eyes to my lips. "I might think of better things to do with our time if you refuse to surf."

"Is that right?" I moisten mine and straighten. "Such as?"

He bends so his lips almost touch mine. "Wineries to visit."

His eyes glint in amusement before he hops into the Jeep. I'm laying bets that's not what he means.

CHAPTER FOURTEEN

Guy's loud exuberance continues for the rest of the day with repeated blow-by-blow accounts of his jump. I tease him and he laughs; but thankfully, Guy drops his insistence I start my surfing lessons. We head to a nearby winery for lunch, sit beneath the metal canopy outside the cafe on wooden benches, and share an afternoon amongst the tall grapevines. Guy relaxes into chatting about the times he's spent here in the past, and I steer the conversation away from his enthusiasm for the local surf scene in case he jumps back to that topic and attempts to drag me for the lesson I agreed to.

I can't remember the last time I was this relaxed and happy, and I push away the darker niggling thought about Guy's future, and follow his mantras instead. *Live for now. Be in the moment.* Sharing these moments with a man who today looks at me as if I'm the most important person in his world both thrills and disquiets me. If only we could stay in this time and place longer – a week, a month. Forever.

The house is cool when we return, the quiet emptiness welcome after the busy afternoon amongst tourists. Guy throws his car keys on the low table near the front door and I head upstairs to change. My pulse rate picks up as I hear his footsteps on the wooden staircase behind. As the afternoon progressed, we moved closer physically and the subtle touches became snatched kisses until only the heat of the day prevented us cuddling together completely.

In the bedroom, I make my way to the open balcony doors. The sea breeze blows into my face and I close my eyes, tuning my senses to the calming sound and scents of nature. The calm ocean laps the beach across the road, with no swell on the water. The afternoon sun heats the bedroom; I pull the curtains across the doors but the sunlight shines through the thin blue material. I'm facing away from the bedroom doorway and my skin goose bumps at the awareness of Guy entering the room.

"Closing out the world?" he asks from behind.

"Taking back the day."

Gentle fingers push my hair from my neck, and a shiver runs through as Guy places his lips on my skin. "A trip to a winery wasn't on our bucket list."

"Why does that matter?"

"Another step away from travelling companions, Phe."

I pull away and turn to look at him. "I think the kiss last night was a bigger step away."

In a sudden movement, Guy seizes my head and his mouth crashes on mine. I gasp, ready to push him away, but who am I kidding, I've waited for this all afternoon. I slide my hand to the nape of his neck and hold him steady, pressing myself into him. Guy backs me against the wall and pushes his tongue into my mouth. We kiss deeply until , struggling to breathe, I wrench my head away.

Guy holds my face steady with his lips remaining close to mine. He studies me with the mix of desire and affection I've seen in his eyes all day, "We don't have to go back to Perth tonight, we can stay until tomorrow. Spend the night together."

"I thought you said you were waiting for me to call the shots."

He arches a brow. "If you don't, I will. We're outside life again, Phe. Living for what we want and I want you."

"Not a travelling companion?" I run my fingertips along his lips.

"I want to carry on this journey with you, yes; but I want us. Don't you think sex would enhance the experience?"

My eyes widen at his forthright words. "That's so romantic," I say sarcastically.

Guy slides his arms around my waist and pulls me into his hips. I stumble and place a hand on his chest. "Unless you don't want to?"

I refuse to overthink this, I'll let my body make the decision on this one. The strength of the arms around me, the solid muscle I'm held against are enough of a temptation for me.

Guy misreads my hesitation. "But I understand if you need a man to love you before you take that step."

"I don't think I'm able to allow myself close to anybody yet," I whisper. "Physically is fine, not emotionally."

He tips my chin. "I promise you'll have respect from somebody who cares about you and is exclusively yours, but we don't have to fall in love."

"Sounds good to me."

Guy pushes a hand beneath my singlet top and draws a finger along my stomach, triggering vibrations from my belly downward. "So we're good?"

"I hope we will be," I say with a giggle. Recklessness, I can do this. What's wrong with a girl wanting no-strings sex?

I pull Guy closer, push my hands beneath the sleeves of his t-shirt, and dig my nails into the hard muscle. He places his lips on mine, sending a wave of sensation through my body, and the last doubt slips away. I'm lost the moment his mouth touches mine, the inexplicable connection fusing us. Guy runs his tongue along my bottom lip and I part my mouth, allowing him to kiss me deeply. Losing my grasp on anything but the warmth of Guy and the growing heat between us, I grip his hair and return his passion.

Guy moves to kiss my neck, his day's scruff scraping along the skin firing heat to the centre of me. He pulls me to him by my hips and slides his hand up my back. The way our bodies shape against each other pulls us into our intense world where nobody else exists. Unable to breathe, I pull away but his grip around my waist tightens.

Guy places his forehead on mine, his breath heating my skin. "You want to do this?"

"Do you?"

Guy laughs. "I'm male, Phe, that's a bloody stupid question." He pulls his t-shirt over his head, confirming the tanned muscles from my fantasies live up to reality. I do the same and Guy's gaze drops to my lace-covered breasts. For a moment we stand on the edge of the precipice, denying this could be just a random hook up. The sexual energy existing between us is underpinned by a current of something else, the polarisation of life and death.

I'm alive because of Guy.

He sits on the edge of the bed and watches me through darkening eyes before holding his arms out. "Come here."

I sit astride Guy, and he reaches behind me to unclasp my bra. I slide my arms from the straps and drop the lacy material to the floor. Continuing to look at me, Guy traces fingers from my side to my breasts, brushing my nipple with his thumb. I hold Guy's head and nip his bottom lip and he rewards me with another breath-snatching kiss, shifting his hands to my ass and digging his fingers into the cotton of my shorts. His arousal pushes between the barrier of our clothes; the heat gathers between my legs at each touch and kiss.

"It's hard to keep my self-control around you," he growls.

"Don't then."

"Don't?" he asks and raises a brow.

Teasingly, I bite the corner of my lip. In a sudden movement, Guy stands and flips me over on the bed, kneeling above. Normally I'd feel exposed and nervous but Guy's expression holds a promise I crave for him to keep.

"You trust me?" he asks.

"I trust you, or I wouldn't be lying here half-naked."

Guy loses the concerned lines on his face and shifts back to a lazy smile. "Sounds good to me."

He unbuttons my shorts and I shuffle out of them as he pulls the material from my legs. Guy hungrily takes in the sight of my nakedness and for the first time in my life, I don't feel exposed under a man's scrutiny.

"You're beautiful, Phe," he says, voice hoarse. "But I think I told you that before."

"Once or twice." I curl a hand into Guy's hair and pull him onto me.

He slowly runs a hand along my leg and the soft touch of his fingers on my inner thigh lights the fuse paper on the need for Guy. I drag my fingers across the ridges of muscle in his back and grip him to me.

"Don't stop kissing me," I say.

Our mouths meet, teeth clashing with the raw intensity of the kiss. Guy takes my wrists in one broad hand, and holds my arms above my head. I make a breathless sound as Guy's rough kisses shift toward my breasts, before he closes his mouth around my hardened nipple. He pushes my legs apart with his knee, fingers travelling up my inner thigh until he discovers my wet heat.

Guy strokes, teasingly, gently. As my arousal grows, he slips a finger inside, and I move against him, pushing myself against the palm of his hand. He slides his tongue across my breasts, teasing my nipples into peaks before pulling one into his mouth. I drown in the sensation of his attention to my body; his expert kisses and touch bringing me to the brink and then pausing, until I can't take the building pressure anymore.

"Guy!" I jerk against his grip on my hands, desperate to touch him too.

Guy hesitates and looks down at me. "You want me to stop?"

"No. Yes. I mean stop doing *that*."

"Why?" He releases my hands and slides his other under my ass, pulling me closer. My body tingles with arousal as his hot mouth finds mine again. I still his hand. "Tell me."

I'm partially entwined around Guy but I want to be naked beneath him and be completely surrounded by his warm strength. Now my hands are free, I move them to the waistband of his shorts and slide my fingers inside. "Why do you think?"

"Oh, right." He lifts himself off me with a smug smile. "Just a sec." Guy pulls his wallet from his pocket and takes out a condom, then shuffles the shorts down. He sits on the bed and passes me the package. "You're going to be in control of this, Phe."

Control. I blink; this is a bigger challenge than choosing which menu to eat from. "What if I say I won't?"

"Then I put my clothes back on." He arches a brow, amusement playing at the corner of his lips. I purse mine, already past my personal point of no return, and take the wrapper from him, tearing it open and rolling the condom onto his hard length.

Guy lies back on the bed and pulls me onto him then. The challenge in his expression is unmistakable. *He means really in control.*

"Okay," I say and settle my hips over his, aware of my slick heat sliding against his firm body. Guy inhales sharply and grips my ass.

As I look down at Guy, my hair falls into his face. He pushes a strand away and his dimpled smile appears. "Hello."

I nudge his nose. "Hello."

As we kiss, my nipples brush against Guy's hard chest, our bodies already slippery with perspiration from the summer heat. Pleasure pulses through as Guy slides against me, but he holds back from pushing inside. I hold his broad shoulders, relaxing into the power Guy's allowing me over him; his strength outweighs mine and he could do whatever he wanted to me, easily. But this is Guy, the man who pulled me from the edge and who hardly needs to ask me to trust him.

Looking down at him, I reach between us and guide him inside. Guy closes his eyes, mouth parted, as I slowly lower myself onto him. His grip on my hips hardens, and I lean forward again, nipping his ear as I rock my hips. Guy says something, but I don't hear, lost in the sensation of him filling me as I move. He groans and reaches a hand between us, rubbing his fingers against me in time with the movements.

Our gazes lock, I drag my hair over my shoulders and continue to slide against him, luxuriating in the pleasure rising with each movement. Suddenly, Guy pushes himself up, and holds me in his lap. I dig my nails into his back and he growls, flipping me over onto the bed, before pausing.

"My turn?" he asks.

As I mouth 'yes', he thrusts hard into me. Guy moves slowly at first, eyes still fixed on mine, before increasing the urgency. The pressure builds as the movement of our bodies sliding together bumps my clit.

I grip his tense shoulders and move against him, unable to pull back from my urgency. Guy kisses me, the movement of his tongue matching the push of his hips. Everything overwhelms into a world of sensation, as I spiral upward toward the edge, to the place where nothing exists apart from pure pleasure. Stars dance in my eyes as I cry out, the ecstasy sending shockwaves through my body, squeezing my heart. Lost in this world, I'm aware of Guy's hips tensing before he thrusts hard into me one more time, swearing as he comes.

Guy wraps his arms tightly around me and buries his head in my neck. I relax back with my eyes closed as our hearts beat against each other. Sticky beneath the sheets, I push them down, wrapping the cotton around my waist as I rest my cheek on Guy's damp chest. I close my eyes and run a finger along his skin. The steady thud of Guy's heart slows as he strokes my hair, soothing me further. I haven't felt as close to anybody for years – if ever – and I barely know him. Disconnecting my emotions from a physical relationship and not worrying about where things will lead brings in a freedom I didn't think I'd enjoy.

"Travelling with you will be a lot more fun now." Guy kisses my damp hair.

Until we reach his final destination.

CHAPTER FIFTEEN

I sit on the kitchen counter and watch as Guy turns last night's leftovers into a meal, throwing in sauces and spices he finds in a cupboard. The water bubbles as he adds the pasta and my stomach growls.

"You okay?" he asks, rubbing a hand on my leg.

"I know we're living in the now, but I worry."

He frowns. "Don't worry. Why worry?"

"About you."

"When I'm with you, I forget about life. Isn't it the same for you?"

Our step into a sexual relationship doesn't mean we need to share everything about ourselves, but the closeness demands I know more. "Yes, but even if you don't want to tell me the whole story, I need to know what's happening to you. I feel like I only know half of you."

"What do you want to know?" He studies the contents of the pan and stirs.

"What do you think?"

"I dunno. Could be anything."

Is he being deliberately evasive here? I take a deep breath. I've felt the strength of this man, but I've also seen the Guy whose pain surfaced briefly last night.

"Do you think you're at the stage you can tell me yet?" I ask.

"About what?"

I swallow. "About what's killing you."

Guy carefully places the spoon on the kitchen counter. "I thought I could get away with that." He looks up with a small smile. "But I understand you want to know."

"And I understand that you don't want to talk about your illness, but I'm asking as your friend –"

"And lover."

"As somebody who cares."

He regards me for a few moments and I worry that I've pushed things too far. "Fine, but will you tell me what happened to you? The full story about your family?"

It's my turn to look away. An exchange of secrets, of things we attempt to hold outside of the place we've created together. "I'm not sure I can."

"Brain tumour."

The words spring from nowhere and I snap my head up. "Oh." I've rehearsed a reaction for the day Guy inevitably told me and that pathetic response wasn't my plan. How can he expect me to react reasonably, when he throws the words out like this then continues to cook as if he asked me to pass him the salt? "Sorry."

"Yeah." He rubs a hand across his short hair. "Of the inoperable variety. Well, they did years ago. Tried to take out what was in there and thought they had. Came back." As he speaks, Guy looks directly at me but his face is impassive. How anybody could come to terms with the fact they're facing death and act nonchalantly I don't know. When I looked death in the face, I was in a haze and welcomed the idea. Is his choice to ignore because he can't fight?

"Are you in pain?"

"Sometimes."

"You said your illness didn't affect you physically.

I thought brain tumours did that."

"Everybody's different, Ophelia."

I tense at him using the name, a warning to stop asking more. "Right."

"Which is why I'm planning everything quickly. I need to organise my trip to the UK."

Brain tumour. I picture him unable to walk, talk… "But in a few months will you be able to?"

"Yes, but the sooner the better. July?"

"I guess. I'll ask for leave and see how things go." "Cool."

At this moment, all I want is to hold Guy, the tears threatening to spill, but I don't think sympathy is what he wants. The sadness I have for him mingles with relief he's finally told me, that he trusts me. I understand now why he never wanted to vocalise the truth.

"Your turn," he says. "Tell me about your family."

I can't be as laid back on the surface as Guy can; the memories too close. I have a condensed version of the story, one I use on the rare occasions I'm forced to tell. Passed from psych to doctor to counsellor in a merry go round as a teen, I have honed my version of the story. Factual. Short. Quick.

"My dad drugged my family and drove the car into a river. Everybody died. Apart from me. Obviously. They think he put sedatives in something we ate or drank that afternoon and my mum and brother passed out on the journey. In the car, between when we left home and he drove into the water, I vomited. My dad was angry with me, really angry, and now I know why. I vomited up the drugs. I knew what he was doing when the car hit the water."

Guy watches silently; and for once, he's unable to respond. "When the car submerged, I tried to help my little brother, but I barely had time to save myself. I was lucky. Even though it was late at night and we were somewhere quiet, another car passing saw the accident happen. A man I've never seen since saved my life." I wipe at my eyes, annoyed a tear has found its way out. "At least my mum and brother didn't know because they were... asleep. My dad must've been conscious before he drowned because there were no drugs in his system. Some days I'm glad he suffered."

"And you feel guilty," says Guy softly.

"Yes. Always. I should've died when I was eleven, shouldn't be here."

"But you are," he whispers. "Strong, beautiful, and capable of more than you realise. Live the life you've been given, that's what your mum would've wanted."

"That's the problem, I am, and I hate it. When I was growing up, before she died, she would talk about how smart I was, how I'd achieve so much. Now I have to, because success is my legacy to her."

Guy shakes his head and takes both of my hands in his, returning me from the edge of my memories to him. "No. You're wrong. Your mum would've wanted you to live a life of colour, not still drowning in the darkness after all these years."

"But I want to. I want to be successful, to be somebody."

"You are somebody. Whatever you choose to do, you will be amazing." Guy takes my face in his hands and looks me straight in the eyes. "Don't sell yourself short."

I place my hands over Guy's, ignoring the growing anxiety. One moment we say we'll be no-strings and the next we tighten the thread that connects us. A tragedy in the past and the threat of death, the guilt that follows.

"I'm going to teach you how to be Ophelia," he says. "You can't be Lia again, but you don't have to be Phe."

"And I'm going to teach you that you don't have to go through things on your own."

He kisses my forehead. "I know, because I have my travelling companion."

He turns back to the pan, stirring with the spoon in one hand and holding my hand in his other. Relaxed, natural, average couple when we're anything but. Secrets revealed, bodies shared, is there any way we can prevent ourselves becoming enmeshed?

CHAPTER SIXTEEN

When I arrived home from Dunsborough, Jen was cagey, and after a couple of days she confronted me – once she'd had a couple of glasses of wine. When I told Jen what Guy had told me about his mother, she shut up. The topic hasn't been mentioned since. Jen's disapproval over Guy pisses me off because I never tagged her as a judgmental person and she has no understanding of our situation.

I spend less time at my share house and tread the waters of a relationship with Guy. Back in Perth, a flurry of texts from Guy descend in the daytime and we catch up in the evening every other day at least. Already we've edged from bucket list 'meetings' to what normal people would term as dates. Within two weeks, I'm free falling into Guy faster than he did through the Australian sky.

Tonight we meet at Guy's place with the pretence we'll discuss the lists and fool ourselves this is the main connection between us. We sit at Guy's table in his shining kitchen with large glasses of wine and his laptop.

"This weekend, I thought we'd tackle one of your bucket list items," says Guy.

"Do I get to choose?" *Not surfing.*

He shrugs. "Sure. I've been researching everything. I've even taken a leaf out of your supremely organised book and begun to plan a timetable of what we can do when."

"Then we probably need to discuss what you're planning." I am not going back to people organising my life for me.

"Sure. I meant I've found places and opening times, no point pinning down further than that before talking to you." He drinks, looking at me over the top of his wine glass. "Apart from the overseas trip."

"Right."

Guy pulls up bookmarked websites on his laptop and talks me through his research. The old enthusiasm is back; the man on the beach who reached out to me has been submerged again.

He clicks to the next page, a tourist page for a town between the sea and the desert. "One of yours. Sleep beneath the stars."

"I hope you don't mean literally sleep under the stars."

Guy laughs. "I'll take a tent, don't panic." He clicks around the site, opening a new page. "Here. To prove there's a real-life campsite we can stay at."

"Okay." I stand and hold out my hand for his wine glass; when he passes me it, his fingers touch mine. Since the sex, the way Guy looks at me is different. I expected him to switch back to casual but respectful, as if we'd done nothing but kiss, but something has shifted. This difference isn't only the line we crossed physically a couple of weekends ago, but a deeper understanding from revealing more than each other's skin.

The sex hasn't been repeated despite catching up for what we deny are dates, but the gathering need between us intensifies with each look or touch. Brushing fingers with Guy immediately triggers a shockwave of arousal inconsistent with such an innocent gesture. He curls his hand around mine and rubs the back for a moment, his shift in expression a nodded understanding he shares my need.

"When do you want to camp?" I ask as I pour the wine.

"Soon? You know I don't want to waste time."

"Sounds fun."

He takes the glass I offer and looks up at me. "Your face doesn't say that."

"I've never been camping, that's all."

Guy wraps his arm around my legs and rests his head against my hip, surprising me with his relaxed intimacy. "You'll have fun!

"Sure…" I stroke his hair. "Where do you want to go to subject me to this?"

"North." He pulls open a bookmarked page with photographs of a star-filled sky above monolithic rocks in the desert. "Pinnacles."

"That isn't too far, is it?"

"A few hours drive. We'll take a weekend off." Again the look. The unsaid: remember what we did on our last weekend?

"In a tent?"

"In a tent." He shifts his hand and rubs my ass. "Don't underestimate the fun you can have in a tent."

I widen my eyes in response to the words and the sudden vision of climbing on top of Guy and asking him not to demonstrate what he's suggesting, but he isn't looking at me anymore.

"Weird." He points at the laptop screen.

"What's weird?"

"Ever since I started researching, I keep finding pictures and ads on other sites I visit, for exactly the thing I looked at. Like this. Dolphin cruises."

"Oh! Dolphins. How about that instead of the camping?" I peer at the screen. "That's normal. Everything you search is likely to reappear as ads."

"How?"

"I guess the internet just stalks us." I laugh but Guy doesn't. "Besides, sometimes the ads are helpful."

"How do they stalk us?"

"I'm not sure. I guess your search history is communicated to advertising sites. Cookies or something."

He closes the lid. "I don't think I like that. Can I stop it happening?"

"Not sure. There might be something on your browser you can use, I don't know."

"So some random company can see everything I look for on the internet?"

"Why? Something to hide?" I tease.

Guy shakes his head, but his face is concerned. "Nothing at all. I don't like being watched, that's all."

"Nobody's watching you."

He wheels his chair back and pulls me onto his lap. "I saw something on TV about how the government wants ISPs to give up people's search history details. Is that what's happening? Bloody weird."

"That's crime related. I don't think we're quite at the Big Brother point in history yet."

"But still."

I wrap my arms around Guy's head, pulling him close, aware that by doing this his face is close to my breasts, and the top I'm wearing is cut low enough to see the swell. He turns his head and places his lips gently on the skin at the top of my breasts, then rubs my back. This physical contact we've avoided isn't helping the arousal that begins instantly with him.

He looks up at me. "Are you going home soon?"

"Why? Do you want me to?"

"No, but you always start watching the clock around 10pm and run home before I think the evening's finished. Are you sure you're not Cinderella?"

I kiss his forehead, knowing if this conversation continues I won't be going home. "I have to wake up early for work."

He sighs and shifts so I have to stand. "One day, I'll make you let go of everything and lose yourself. The world still functions without your control, you know."

I wrinkle my nose at his typical honesty. "Yeah, I get it. I'm a control freak. I'm working on that thanks to the fact you point out I am on a regular basis."

"So stay." He reaches out and takes my hand.

"I haven't planned to."

"You can borrow my toothbrush."

I shake my head at him, tempted. "I don't know."

He drags me back down onto his lap and holds my waist. "Let's stop this, Phe."

"Stop what?"

"Since the night in Dunsborough, I've obsessed about you. You've stolen every rational thought from my head and replaced them with dreams of you. And I'm confused because I'm not sure what you want." He nuzzles my neck. "I think you want more, but you're guarded and I can't tell."

My heart skips a beat in my chest. "I wasn't sure what you wanted."

"Seriously, Phe? Do you think I'd say no, if you told me you wanted more?"

"But this is confusing; we've moved from friends to potential lovers and —"

He breaks into one of his grins. "*Potential?* I think we've gone beyond that."

"I mean potentially lovers, not a one night thing." I frown at his teasing.

"Oh, no way is one night enough. Not with you." Guy edges his hands beneath my shirt, stroking my belly with soft fingers triggering the aching heat between my legs. "I have day-long visions of you naked. I need to check those visions are accurate."

"Is that right?"

"Yes, so if you could take your clothes off and get into my bed that would be helpful." I make a mock-gasp and grab his hand. He tugs his brow together. "Or did I put you off last time? Is that what's wrong?"

Memories of his hands and mouth on my skin, and switching off the world for one of our own, edge me closer to giving in to him. He places soft kisses along my neck, hands sliding along my side and pushing up my t-shirt.

"No, you didn't put me off. Why would you think that?"

"You're a closed book. Stay," he says, mouth moving against the sensitive hollow of my neck.

I shiver. *Sensible, Phe. Work.* "I can't."

"Wrong answer." Guy pushes my top higher and I grab his hand, but he pushes my fingers away. "Come on. Stay. I can't promise you'll sleep much though."

"That's the problem!" I protest but allow him to remove my shirt.

Guy moistens his lips as he looks at me. I'm unable to pull back from the physical us, the crackle of the energy arcing between and drawing us together. Since the weekend at Dunsborough, when we're together, we touch constantly: lacing fingers, stroking skin, anything to keep a grip on what we have.

"Okay, Prince Charming," I whisper and rest my head on his.

Guy stands, keeping hold of me and I wrap my legs around his waist. "Shush. I told you, no princes." He kisses me leisurely, his lips soft and teasing against mine. "Go for the Big Bad Wolf instead."

I nip his bottom lip, wishing he wouldn't stop. "Big Bad Wolf?"

"Oh, yeah." He heads toward the stairs, still gripping me to him. "He sees you better, hears you better, and eats..."

"Ohmigod!" I laugh and put my hand over his mouth.

Guy's eyes shine and he twists his head away from my hand. "You're staying. End of story."

Lisa Swallow

CHAPTER SEVENTEEN

When I have the nightmares, they follow me into the daylight every time. I've learned to block the memories and blank my mind, but the anxiety triggered by my subconscious doesn't subside for hours. On those days, my world is shrouded in red; I'm on constant alert against threats to my peace of mind. When these days coincide with negative experiences at work, things spiral.

I see the change happening, as if standing outside and watching the anxious Phe unable to focus, making endless lists or staring into space. I recognise her and hate when she slips back in. I don't want her here but know she's hard to shake again.

Time with Guy switches off the anxiety; but away from Guy, things magnify and this worries me. Who am I lying to more when I say this is no-strings, no real connection – him or me?

The afternoon in Dunsborough, when I told Guy I only wanted something physical, I fully intended to follow through. I didn't expect to feel anything apart from purely sexual pleasure. Then I told myself this was a one-off, a release of pent-up frustration and emotions from months of control. Wrong. Each time we have sex, I'm drawn closer to Guy. The physical connection is different than before; nobody has looked me in the eyes or spoken to me when lost in the physical intensity. Yes, I have Guy's

132

care and respect; but in his eyes, I see more. Something is winding around us, each time tying me tighter to Guy in a way which can only be unhealthy.

This is how the fear creeps in, over the loss I'm facing. We don't speak about Guy's illness, in the same way he doesn't probe me about my mental state. I've attempted to research his condition on the internet; but I was met with a confusing array of symptoms and varieties of brain tumours. One thing is certain: Guy will become affected physically.

We fool ourselves we're living in the now, but our lives are focused on what lies ahead. I'm not sure I can cope with a bright future turning black again. I tell myself I'm stronger, that I'm walking into this with my eyes wide open, but my heart is open and exposed too.

Through Guy I'm learning I don't have to remain frozen in a moment, or controlled by the past, and that my reliance on medication only to change my life is wrong. He echoes suggestions I've been told for years, painting a holistic picture of my recovery. Guy persuades me to attend yoga classes with him and join him for walks at the weekends. We're no longer travelling companions; we're companions. Lovers. A couple.

I attempt to back away and pull at the binds, but they're too tight. I need to see this through to the end.

CHAPTER EIGHTEEN

#2 Sleep Beneath The Stars

The red dust and long roads point us in the direction of the Pinnacles. The West Australian sky holds nothing but the sun, some times of the year no clouds appear for weeks. This'll make stargazing beautiful. The further we travel from the city, the more relaxed I become, the hum of the engine and Guy's music pushing in a holiday atmosphere. I position the aircon to blow across my face and sit back, eyes closed.

"How was your week?" asks Guy.

"Pretty good. I spoke to Pam about writing another article and she said she'd think about publication."

"What's the article about?"

I side glance him. "Mental health issues."

"Hmm." Guy taps the steering wheel. "Great you asked her, but do you feel up to re-visiting that kind of thing?"

"Why wouldn't I?"

"Tapping into things you're hiding, Phe, could trigger something."

I look out of the window, at the red sand and scrub landscape. We could be in the same place we were an hour ago because nothing's changed. "I'm fine. You know I am. I want to do this and I asked which was a big thing for me!"

"Sorry. I worry about you."

"That's sweet and very perceptive; but if you're going to teach me to be more assertive, I'll apply the new attitude to you too."

"Oh, really?" Guy arches a brow and glances at me.

"Yes. So be quiet."

Guy chuckles. "So, you haven't camped before?"

"No. Not sure I'll like it."

"You can always sleep in the Jeep if you hate sleeping in a tent that much."

"Isn't the bucket list idea that we do things we never have before?"

"True. Yours intrigue me, as if you're setting yourself challenges rather than doing things you enjoy."

I know.

"You don't think I'll enjoy sleeping under the stars?"

"Not if you don't like camping."

"How about you? Do you camp much?" I ask.

"Not as much as I used to." Guy launches into stories about camping as a child, then later as a teen. I picture the younger Guy with the friends he mentions, and wonder why he spends so much time alone.

The campsite is located in a small town with little else than a few cafes and basic shops, much of the place geared towards tourism. We head off the road through the gates of the campsite, the bright blue ocean a few hundred metres away past the chalets and tent pitching sites. Guy disappears into the reception area and I wait.

"Have you ever seen the Pinnacles?" asks Guy as he hops back into the Jeep. "We could stop there first?"

"I've heard of them."

"You don't sound keen."

"Shouldn't we pitch the tent or whatever before

the sun goes down? Go tomorrow instead?"

"You are a very practical lady, Phe. Maybe we can sneak in the National Park at night, or close by anyway. The stars will be unreal there."

We have an ample choice of spaces with amazing beachfront sites; the tourist season has all but ended. I hang back as Guy pulls all the camping gear from the back of the Jeep. He tips the canvas from the bag and shakes the tent into place; the muscles in his arms and shoulders flexing as he does. His singlet top is cropped at the arms, revealing the edge of his tanned chest coupled with his board shorts low on his hips. My sexy, Aussie surfer Guy.

Guy straightens. "Are you going to help or just stare at my awesome body?"

"Ha, ha." I pick up a canvas bag and tip pegs onto the floor, then look at Guy in despair.

He shakes his head. "You've missed out if you've never camped before."

"Not quite the accommodation my grandparents liked."

"So no school camp?" Guy grabs a couple of pegs and mallet, setting about securing the tent.

"Once, but we were in chalets." I indicate the row of wooden, blue buildings behind us.

"Right. Would you have preferred that?"

"No. I have to sleep under the stars to tick off the list. Or in a tent at least."

He grins and throws the mallet in the air, then catches. "Exactly."

With little help from me, Guy finishes putting up the tent. Inside are two small sleeping sections and a space between where Guy has dumped cooler of food and drink. I haul my newly purchased sleeping bag from the car and Guy appears next to me to lug my bag out.

"Glad to see you're travelling light."

"I don't need much for one night camping."

"I bet you wrote a list," he says with a half-smile.

"And ticked everything off."

"Didn't you?"

"Nah, just threw stuff into the car."

"How do you know you haven't forgotten anything?"

Guy takes my face in both hands, blue eyes searching mine. "I have the important things and I'm with you, so what else matters?"

He retrieves two low camping chairs from the boot of the jeep and puts them up. "For you." He gestures and I sit.

The lawned tent pitching areas stretch toward the beach, thinning to sand a few hundred metres away. An ocean breeze blows through the late afternoon heat, carrying the ozone scent and call of the seagulls. I close my eyes and breathe deeply.

Peace.

"This unscrambles things, don't you think?" he asks.

I open an eye to where Guy has taken the other seat and sits looking toward the beach too. "This place is peaceful."

"No city, no traffic, just nature. I think people relax because places like this empty our minds. Reality is so far away and can't intrude."

"I guess."

"Here is living, there, the city, is existing, don't you think?"

"Then you should move out here if you don't have to work. Spend your days surfing and whatever else you like."

"I'd love to but there are things holding me to the city. Especially now." He reaches across and takes my hand, and we sit in the strange peace we create, silently.

****

The nearby national park is a true desert, the ancient rock structures rising from the sand and towering above. I'd seen pictures but never realised how many of the jagged pillars were here, there're thousands stretching across the desert. Amongst them, weathered low rocks with rounded tops look uncomfortably like tombstones. Alone in the eerie landscape, I wander with Guy through the taller rocks, gripping his hand.

We head to the lookout point, Guy eager to show me the sun drop behind the weathered spires. Sunset happens quickly in this part of the world, a sudden drop of the sun throws the world into darkness within minutes. Here, that darkness is preceded by a spectacular array of sunset colours, the rocks lit in front of a backdrop of burnt orange and deep red.

Lost in the beauty of the scene in front of me, I rest against the bonnet of the Jeep, barely noticing Guy's arm around my waist.

"Now we sneak away to find the stars," he says, drawing me closer.

We drive slowly into the shadows, and Guy cuts the engine. For a moment, I stare at the stars emerging from the dying sunset and soon they're streaming above the alien landscape. The Martian feel to the place leaves me unsure if I'll be able to breathe when I leave the car.

The door closes as Guy climbs out, breaking my reverie. I follow and the humid air filled with the scent of the sandy earth is breathable after all.

"Climb on the roof," suggests Guy.

"The roof?"

"Yeah." He clambers up and hangs his legs in front of the windscreen, holding a hand out. I join him, the warm metal sticking to my bare legs.

On the roof, we're not much closer to the stars but surrounded by a canopy dropping to the ground behind the stones. Guy draws his knees to his chest.

"And here we have 'how to feel insignificant

101'," he says.

The purple and blue of the Milky Way leads a pathway through the night sky, bright and surreal; they rise behind the tall rock formation adding to the sensation of sitting on another planet. I tip my head back and the bright stars above fill the darkness and dizzy me.

"You're quiet," says Guy.

"I've never seen anything so beautiful," I whisper. "I can't believe this is so close to where I live."

"Technically, what you're looking at is light years away."

I elbow him. "You know what I mean."

Guy wraps an arm around my shoulder and I shuffle across the roof so he can hold me closer. "How incredibly sad that something so beautiful shines the brightest just before it dies," he says. "Some of the stars are long gone, with the light from their death just reaching us."

"Don't say that." The stars appear to swarm across the sky and I focus, wishing for a shooting star. "The stars aren't all dead."

"New stars are born all the time, there'll be many burning at this moment that we can't see yet because their light hasn't had time to reach us." He laughs softly. "I tell you to forget the past and we're looking straight at it."

"Stop analysing what could be a romantic moment," I say with a sigh.

"Out here we're alone, kissing under the light of thousands of stars." He tips my face toward him and places a gentle kiss on my mouth. "In a world where I'm disconnected from everything but you. Is that romantic?"

"Better." I touch his lips then look around. "We could be on Mars."

"We could, but I'd rather not."

I pull away and lie back attempting to make out the constellations around. "You're right, I do feel disconnected. Looking at what's out there we know nothing about is overwhelming."

"Why are you afraid?" asks Guy as he lies next to me, staring upward too.

"I'm not afraid."

"We're both afraid of life and what it has to offer when really we should just 'be' together."

I twist my head to him. "But you do that. You live for today."

Guy continues to look upward and takes hold of my hand. "Todays like this, yes. Other days, I'm afraid. I worry that I've made another bad decision."

"What about?"

"Lots of things."

I squeeze his hand. "Can we stay with the stars?"

"If tomorrow we can watch the fire of a new dawn." Guy says the words quietly, as if talking to himself.

"Of course."

Rolling onto his side, Guy looks down, shielding me against the sky. "Do I make you feel like living?"

"What a strange question."

"Since the night I met you, you've never mentioned what you almost did. I think you're better now, not cured, but better. What's changed?"

"Medication?" I suggest.

"Acceptance?"

"Of what?"

"That destruction and loss aren't inevitable."

"Why are you always so serious in the dark?" I whisper and touch his cheek.

"Because you can't see me properly."

"I think I see more of you than you realise."

He looks away and doesn't respond for a few moments. "I like that you're living. Really living, like I told you was possible."

"I don't want to think about that night, Guy." I reach out and curl my fingers into his hair. "But I'm glad you were there."

"I would say I'm glad you were there too, but that would sound wrong." My skin tingles where he gently traces my features with his fingers, like a blind man memorising the contours of his lover's face. "I think I was afraid to live too, until recently."

"Because you'll be in pain soon?"

"No, because I don't know what the future holds."

We fall silent, and I attempt to make out his features in the growing darkness. "Do you want to talk about this?"

"No. Sorry. I've no idea why I mentioned anything. Ruining the moment, huh?"

I shift closer, holding my mouth close to his. "Kiss me."

"I will kiss you for as long as the stars shine," he whispers. Guy pulls me close and steadies himself as he slips against the roof.

I giggle. "Or as long as we don't fall off the top of the car."

"Phe, Phe, Phe," he says with a sigh. "The girl who's good for me." He pulls me onto him, so I'm looking down, hair sweeping his face. The land around is silent, the only sound our breathing. Guy's chest rises and falls against mine as I balance on his hard body.

"We could be the last people in this Martian world," I whisper.

He holds my hair from my face and covers my face and mouth with kisses. "I think we probably are."

"Just me and some Guy, in our world of stars."

"You're happy?" he asks.

"Are you?"

"Spectacularly."

We kiss beneath the Milky Way, under the stars burning bright, their frozen moment in time shared with us. The stars' past illuminates our present, and have already lived in a future we may never see.

****

The campsite is quiet and dark when the Jeep rolls to the locked gates. We hop out and Guy takes my hand, leading us to the tent. Guy flicks on an electric lamp hanging in the centre of the tent then sits on one of the sleeping bags.

"Are you sure you don't want to sleep outside?" he asks.

"Very funny."

"Getting naked then?"

Guy drags his t-shirt off and pats the sleeping bag next to him. What else did I expect sharing a tent with him? Sex is part of our deal, and I have no complaints about how good we are together, but the intensity of his lovemaking sometimes worries me. Each time, I'm aware we're drawn tighter together and I'm frightened I'll not be able to let him go. Am I fooling myself already that I can untangle myself from Guy?

"Don't you feel as if you're floating in the world after looking at the stars?" he asks. "I do. I want to touch reality – you – and ground myself back on Earth. Does that sound strange?"

"A little." I sit with him and run my fingers along his chest; smoothing my hands across his shoulders.

"Was I too intense? I think I had a bit of an existentialist moment back there," he says with a laugh. "Kiss me."

I move closer, and we kiss in a way becoming too familiar, Guy's gentleness and understanding pouring from his lips. As usual, he backs this up with something purely sexual and absolutely male.

"Do you know why sex when you're camping is great?" he asks.

"Enlighten me."

"Because it's fucking in tents."

I smack him in the chest and he laughs, catching my arms. Guy holds my arms out of the way as he tugs at my t-shirt, whispering what he's going to do as soon as I take my clothes off and how if I don't remove them, he will. My ability to resist anything Guy ever suggests is poor.

Guy's correct; as always, sex with him is intense. Each time he takes a little more of my soul when his body melds with mine, as if we're reconnecting with something once lost. Guy's use of the word fucking plays in my mind afterwards; is this what he's really doing? Perhaps Guy can deny what's happening and finds closing off his feelings easier than I do.

Later, as I doze in his arms, Guy shifts away. "I'll be right back."

His loss of body heat hits and I snuggle further into the sleeping bag, against the hard ground, as I tug the smooth material up to my nose. I'm drowsy when the tent zips closed a few minutes later, at the point between sleeping and waking when moving is too much effort.

"Phe?"

I don't reply. Guy shuffles around and then his warm body settles next to mine. He strokes my hair then kisses my forehead, impossibly sweet when that's the last thing he was ten minutes ago.

"Bad decisions," he says in a low voice. Who is he talking to? Me or himself? Guy shifts again and I hear him sigh, the comfort of his body against mine lost as he lies away from me.

We say so much to each other yet so little, on the edge of each other's lives. He tells me I'm his, but I don't think he's mine.

CHAPTER NINETEEN

We sit at the table outside the cafe where we first met. Technically, the second time. Each time we come here, whoever arrives first selects this table. Less than two months and we have our own place. What next? A song? Pet names?

Guy's in one of his distracted moods, the days he isn't tactile. I'm learning that he's one extreme to another. Quiet and introspective, a force field around himself, or open and gregarious, sweeping everyone into his enthusiasm. I take these mood changes in my stride, understanding his desire to keep things hidden from others.

The morning after the star gazing, Guy wasn't around when I woke, and he returned half an hour later from a beach walk. He was back to his bright cheerful self and no longer the serious man in the dark. Guy chatted about our trip to the Pinnacles and after a quick breakfast, we packed up and went home.

This is the first time we've seen each other since, and even though I was busy at work and tired, I couldn't figure out if this week's absence is deliberate. His current mood isn't helping. Guy plays with the edge of his watch and when the meeting descends into conversations about the weather, I decide to push.

"How are you, Guy? You're quiet."

"What do we do next?" He lifts his eyes to mine.

"I don't know, I... Where do you want this to go?"

"No, on the list, Phe." He frowns. "Why? Are you worried about this between us?"

"No, should I be?"

"You know why. Because I'll be gone soon."

I shift in my seat and glance at the couple behind Guy, holding hands, heads together sharing a joke. The elephant in the room is about to trample everything.

"That's for me to deal with," I say stiffly. "But this is a shadow I don't want over us. Over you."

He lifts a hand to push hair from his face that's no longer there, a habit that's hard to kill, then sips on his coffee instead. I pray he's not going to start a conversation about the negative again.

"Can I choose the next item on the lists?" he asks.

"You chose last time."

"Fine. You choose. There aren't many we can still do locally so we should start our plans to go away."

I nod, not only are we stepping further into each other's lives, but out of the world we're in.

"I'm curious why so many things on your list are ordinary," he says. "I'd expect you to have more imagination."

"They may be ordinary to you, but there're things on the list that are a huge step outside of the ordinary for me," I retort.

"Not just because this way you're sure you'll achieve them all?"

I sit back and cross my arms. "What about surfing?"

"Easy."

"For you."

"Easy to achieve, I can teach you less than half an hour from where you live, hardly a big ticket item."

Images of myself in the water trigger the anxiety, in turn pushing irritation with Guy's dismissal of something huge to me. "Just because you already surf! Surfing can still be a big deal to someone else! I don't mock your list items!"

"Sorry." Guy's long fingers curl around my hand and he squeezes.

We sit in silence for a few moments, Guy's hand circling mine. I stare at the coffee rings on the table, at my hands, at the people around. Anywhere but at him.

"It's the water, isn't it, Ophelia?" he asks. "You don't like water. I noticed at the beach."

"I can swim."

"But you don't want to?"

I pull my hand from under his and sit on my hands. "Because of what happened to me. My family drowned and I nearly did, remember?"

"Right."

I look up at him, shocked at his nonchalance. "Did you hear what I said?"

"Your family drowned and you nearly did, so naturally you're scared of going underwater. You told me before. I get it."

"You 'get it'. Don't you think this is a big deal to me?"

"Phe, people poke and prod at others to spill their thoughts and fears. If you wanted to talk about this, you would, I'm not asking you to."

"But you're so cold about what's so difficult for me to talk about!"

"What do you want me to say? I'm sorry for your loss? Well done on getting out? Phe, if you want to talk to somebody about what happened, I'll listen."

Each word he says pushes my anxiety higher, anger building that he doesn't care. "Wow. Thanks." I stand. "I have to get back to work."

Guy doesn't move or attempt to touch me and before he can respond, I storm away.

Usually when memories of the day the water stole my family emerge, I'm dragged back and prepared for the inevitable nightmares. Today the thoughts are funnelled into anger instead. I didn't want platitudes or concerned looks, but I didn't expect him to be this dismissive over the fear the situation causes.

****

Guy's reaction circles my mind for the rest of the afternoon, dragging my thoughts back to the bordering argument every time there's a lull in my work. I question my decision to allow him close, to want him and all the doubts over whether this relationship should go ahead. Then I worry I'm overreacting; but when the fear is triggered, it sweeps logic away.

The cloud of frustration hangs over me the whole way home on the bus, my patience with being jostled by strangers leading me to growling at them.

This is bad. I'm bothered by what Guys says and does. Really bad. Head bowed against the possibility of eye contact with anybody, I step off the bus.

Guy waits at the bus stop, beneath the metal roof, a bunch of pink flowers in his hand. I stop dead and step out of the way of the flow of bodies.

"Flowers on special offer again, were they?" I ask snidely. "Looking for a random girl to give them to?"

"No. I bought them for you. I want to explain."

A young woman throws me a curious look as she passes, then lingers her gaze on Guy before looking back to me and raising an eyebrow.

"About what?"

"Why I reacted like I did to what you told me."

The bus door hisses closed behind me and the smell of diesel accompanies the bus's departure. Guy holds the flowers out to me. "Don't throw them off a cliff this time."

The cellophane crinkles as I take hold of the pink roses. His half-smile pisses me off. "I didn't throw them. I kicked them."

Guy steps forward, placing his fingers lightly on my cheek. "Sorry, Phe. I don't want to upset you."

His concern is genuine; his gesture an apology made in front of giggling school kids and amused looks from passersby. Why do this in public?

"Come back to mine and talk," I say.

He scrunches his nose. "Am I welcome? Jen thinks I'm a psycho."

"She does not!"

"I heard her say that!"

"I don't care what she thinks."

Guy wraps an arm around my shoulders as we set off to my place. "That's an improvement for you. You care what everybody thinks."

I could retort that I don't, but he's correct. Or he was.

The house echoes as I close the door.

"I tell you what, I'll cook. A peace offering," he says.

I rub my head in confusion, at his barrelling in and taking over my evening when I'm still pissed off with him. "You don't need to do that. I invited you in to talk."

"We can talk too. I want to take care of you. You worked and I didn't do anything today apart from piss you off."

Take care of me? I indicate the rainbow of stains on his fingertips. "You painted today."

"I like to switch my mind off sometimes. Especially when people mention death."

Guy's expression freezes me in the moment; and with that, I let go of my anger, guilt worming its way in instead. "Oh. Crap. Sorry. I didn't think the conversation might upset you too."

He shakes his head. "No, I apologise for triggering whatever I did in you." Guy opens a cupboard and drags out a packet of rice. "What do you have that will go with this?" When I don't respond, he opens the fridge and pokes around inside as if he's a resident. "Is this all your food?"

"A lot is. Jen's spending more time with Cam recently."

"Cute," he remarks. "Poor guy."

"That's bitchy."

He shrugs and sets a tub of sour cream on the counter. "I don't like most people. They make my head hurt."

"But you have friends, I've met them. Not many or often, but they exist."

"Acquaintances. I prefer not to become attached to people." He pulls out a kitchen chair. "Sit."

Confused further, I do as he says and place the still packaged bouquet on the wooden table in front of me. Is he saying in a roundabout way he doesn't want to become attached to me? One of our silences follows as I lose myself in those thoughts and he chops up vegetables.

"Most people," he says after a few minutes, not turning.

"You're confusing," I say.

"I confuse myself on a daily basis." Guy pulls another chair out and sits. "I don't talk about myself and you don't either. That's why I didn't respond earlier. I thought we were the same, that you didn't want me to pry."

"Do you want me to ask you questions?"

"Sometimes, but usually no. As I always say, I want to live for now and not dwell on the future. You need to do the same, but not dwell on the past."

"You worry about the past too, Guy."

He taps the table. "Too much. I like my present. Life's been pretty cool since I met this girl on the edge of her life."

"So we drop the serious?" I ask.

"Unless you want to talk about your family?"

"No."

"No worries, so about the surfing..."

I stare. For a man who can be intuitive, he still holds the ability to surprise me with his crass disregard for my feelings. "Really, Guy?"

"If we're not going to look backwards, let's look forward. You have a fear of water. I want to help you face that. Come on, I jumped out of a plane and I'm terrified of heights!"

"I didn't know that."

Guy shrugs and returns to the steaming pan. "What's the point in a bucket list filled with easy things? You're challenging yourself in everything you have written."

He's looking at the list, re-pinned to the fridge by a magnet, partially obscured by flyers for the local pizza place.

"Not quite everything."

"Hmm."

The meal is joined by relaxed chatting about a new movie we want to see and I push him to tell me more about his experience skydiving. At the time, I never considered Guy could be frightened; there was no hint of nerves when he walked away from me across the field that afternoon.

We cuddle on the sofa, as I lie against Guy's chest and he plays with my hair. Lost in a TV drama for half an hour, Guy surprises me when he speaks.

"This has changed. Us. We're not just physical anymore."

I look up at him. "Is that worrying you?"

"A little." He touches my lips, and I spot the intense Guy returning. "Please don't do it."

"Do what?"

"Fall in love with me."

I swallow, stomach tightening at his words. "I'm not. Won't."

"I care about you too much to let that happen. I

don't want to ruin us. I mean, I probably will anyway, but don't help me."

I take Guy's hand. "Don't do this." *Don't spoil this.* "Let's make the most of our time."

I shuffle around and place my hands on his chest, eager to quieten him with a kiss. "So we had an argument and that pushes us into the 'normal couple' realm; but we're not, and I don't expect us to be. Okay?"

"Okay." The veil of seriousness drops from his eyes, a relief in his expression that unintentionally hurts.

I don't expect us to be a normal couple, but the desire to edges in more each day. I wipe the thought from my mind with a kiss, throwing the inner fears and frustration into a fierce embrace until the thoughts are wiped and replaced by the physical lust I have for him. Denial is easier if the emotion is twisted into a different direction.

CHAPTER TWENTY

Mullaloo Beach is a short drive from my place and Guy picks me up from the house with two surfboards strapped to the roof. We arrive in the car park near the limestone-bricked surf club, and I catch a glimpse of the sparkling Indian Ocean beyond the trees. I grip my hands together as Guy hops out, bashing around as he unstraps the board from the roof. He opens my door. "Ready?"

"No. But let's go."

"We'll take things easy, I promise."

We're not the only surfers on the beach, mid-morning and already a few are pausing for a break; the serious surfers with their wetsuits peeled to their waists sit, drinking and eating. Nearby a group of people line up on boards with an instructor, five boards in a row.

"Hey, man." A man around Guy's age with cropped brown hair nods at Guy as we approach.

"Hey. How's the surf today?" Guy props the worn surfboard in front of him.

"Yeah. Fine. Too busy though." He points at the nearby pupils, a row of people on the sand learning how to stand on a surfboard. A second group is in the ocean, the instructor calling directions at them as they paddle around. "You should've come down early."

"Waited for Phe." I give a small wave to the man sitting on the sand. "Phe, this is Gordy."

Gordy holds his damp hand out and I take hold. His grip is hard as he shakes. "Good to meet you. This your girl, Guy?"

"I guess she is." He slips an arm around my waist. "We were travelling companions."

"You been away?"

"Nah. Soon though."

"Cool."

I shift from foot to foot, gauging the strength of the waves, relieved that closer to shore the break is low. Guy chats to Gordy and I switch off, unable to follow their conversation filled with surf jargon. Before he drags me onto a surfboard and pushes me out to sea, I need to acquaint myself with the water.

I approach the edge of the beach where the warm ocean laps the shore, staring at the foam. The water trails across my sandals and I slip them off, allowing the warm water to touch my feet. The closest I've come to swimming since the accident is ankle deep in water. I had a freak out at school swimming lessons two years after the deaths and have avoided the pool and beach ever since. An Aussie girl scared of the surf; I definitely don't fit the image Guy does.

I look back over to where he chats to a friend, butterflies swarming behind my navel. His appearance is the same as the second time we met, defined muscular legs in blue board shorts and a loose t-shirt across his broad back. His hair is still shorter, a reminder of the other Guy, the one who holds himself at a distance.

As if aware of my inspection, he turns and flashes me a smile before leaving the board and wandering over. "You might have to go a bit deeper than that."

I shove my hands in my shorts pockets. "I know. Is it okay if I just paddle first?"

"Sure. We have all day."

I thrust my bag at him and peel off my shorts and t-shirt, revealing a blue bikini I bought several weeks ago, in a move to tell myself I was going to do this. Guy stares as I unzip the bag and shove my clothes in.

"Jesus, Phe," he says eyes zoning in on my chest.

"What?"

"Good thing I'm holding this bag because I'm thinking about the other evening and the thoughts aren't very clean."

"Well, stop. I'm sure you're used to seeing girls in bikinis."

"Oh, yeah, but you're different."

"I was going to kiss you, but I'm not now," I retort.

"Aww, go on." He puckers his lips.

With a small sigh, I place a hand on his chest and rest my lips briefly on his. "Go put the bag down and stay with me while I'm in the water please."

"Sure thing."

A shirtless Guy returns and takes my hand in his. We wade into the shallows where the waves break against my knees. I can do this, but the idea of the water dragging me under churns fear in my stomach. As we reach the point the water reaches my waist, the movement of the waves threatens to pull my feet from the sand. I grip Guy's arm with both hands.

"Ouch. Watch those nails."

Red marks appear on his arm and I smooth them, with an apology.

A larger wave splashes further up to my chest, and a panicked sound escapes my mouth, as I grasp at Guy again.

"Hey, Phe, Don't worry. Look out at the ocean, the water's calm."

"Then where did that wave come from?"

He smirks. "That wasn't a wave!"

"And that's what bothers me." Every cell in my body screams at me to turn and wade out of the water, but I can't move, swaying in the push and pull of the tide, hanging onto Guy.

"You want to keep going?"

I shake my head, hair flying around my face because words aren't possible. I gasp as my chest tightens.

"Phe, take deep breaths. You're fine."

"I'm not," I manage to squeak out. "Take me back."

"Stay here. Just for a few minutes."

"I can't move and they're coming. Guy, please."

"What's coming? The waves?"

"The memories. I can't do this. I can't let them in." Tears push into my eyes, head aching with the attempt to control them and my voice rises in pitch.

"I've got you." Guy lets go of my hand and wraps me to him. "When was the last time you went in the water?"

"Eight years ago." I shake away the blackness coming in, the breathlessness as the water took me. "Don't. Please. Take me back."

"We're close to shore. Turn round. We can walk back."

"I can't! I can't move!" I suck in a breath, heart skipping out of time and magnifying the anxiety. "Guy!"

"Phe, shh. I'll take you back."

"The sand's sucking me down!"

Guy chews on his mouth and doesn't respond. I'm not surprised; he's in three feet of water with a hysterical woman. In a swift move, he picks me up, arms beneath my damp legs and I wrap my arms around his neck, burying my face into his shoulder. His skin is warm from the sun, scented with the ocean and sunscreen, soothing. I focus on him, on pushing away the memories. How stupid, thinking I could do this all at once.

"I don't think I can surf today," I say into his shoulder.

"You think?" he says with a laugh.

"This isn't funny." We reach the ankle deep water and I become aware of curious onlookers. "God, I'm so embarrassed. Get me out of here."

I struggle against Guy, he drops me to my feet, and I stride back to where he'd left the surfboard and my bag. He catches up as I stumble, on one leg attempting to pull my shorts on.

"Phe…" Guy envelops me in his arms. "You're shaking. I'm so sorry."

I fight to control my breathing, which isn't helped by the fact Guy's gripping me so tightly I can hardly breathe. "I need to get away from here." My voice is muffled against his chest.

"No worries." He delves back into the bag and hands me his car keys. "I'll be with you in a minute."

The ocean mocks me as I watch from the safety of Guy's Jeep, my clothes damp and uncomfortable from where I pulled them over my wet bikini. Calm, blue, and beautiful, the Indian Ocean is part of a paradise other people long to visit, and to me all the place brought was the blackness I avoid.

I'm angry with myself.

Guy appears with the board and his bag, walking barefoot across the car park with sandy feet. I chew a nail, waiting for his teasing, not ready to deal if he's unable to appreciate my situation.

Placing a striped blue and white towel on the seat, Guy climbs in, and looks at me. "You've some colour back in your face."

"Mmm."

"Okay now?"

"I will be."

He closes a hand around mine, the comfort and his understanding soothing. "I overestimated what you could do. Sorry."

"No, don't be. Without you, I wouldn't have got this far."

"I know you feel terrible right now, but what you did was a good thing. Fear. You're feeling." He kisses my forehead; holding his lips on the spot between my eyebrows.

"Feeling? I've felt for a long time."

"But bad feelings. You're dealing with them; that's good. I'm surprised you didn't have a total meltdown." Guy strokes my cheek.

"Being carried back to shore by you wasn't a total meltdown? You have no idea how embarrassed I am by that."

"Not really. I've seen you worse." He looks ahead as he pushes the keys into the ignition.

"I think you like rescuing me," I say.

"Rescuing you? No, you're rescuing yourself. I'm just watching."

"And you. Who's rescuing you?"

"I don't need rescuing."

"I haven't forgotten what you told me a few weeks ago, Guy. You need help with your fears, too."

"I'm not scared of anything apart from hurting you." He doesn't look at me, glancing over his shoulder as he reverses. "We should have lunch. Celebrate what you just did because you're bloody awesome."

As we drive away, my panic recedes the further we move from the beach. I don't believe him – about his fears or about my supposed awesomeness.

CHAPTER TWENTY-ONE

#10 Fall in love

My body aches after dealing with the panic and I'm tired, I want to go home and hide; but instead, we head back to Guy's place.

I like Guy's house – who wouldn't want this level of luxury – but there's an air of sterility to the place. The living areas don't look lived in, everywhere neat and clean. I'm keen on a tidy house; but sharing a place means no possibility of having a home exactly as I'd like, so I don't worry.

"Want to watch some movies this evening?" he asks as he pours himself some water. "Or go out somewhere?"

"How about more planning?" I ask. "Something to take my mind off this morning's disaster."

Guy breaks into a huge grin. "Awesome! Wait until you see what I have."

He disappears and returns with a manila folder. We sit side by side at the counter and Guy pulls out pictures of places he wants to visit. Gradually, he draws me away from the incident on the beach as I look at pictures of London and English landmarks. Perhaps, now it's time to focus on items outside of the ocean-surrounded country

I live in.

I scrawl notes as he flicks through printed research he's completed on hotels and flights, items highlighted in fluorescent colours. "This is thorough, Guy!"

"Truthfully, I've planned this for years. I have folders full of plans starting from when I was a teen."

"You should've done the backpacking thing – Aussie rite of passage, work in a bar in London."

He flicks through the pictures. "I considered going, but there wasn't anybody to take with me."

"I'm sure you're the sort of person who could meet up and make friends pretty easily."

"Sometimes." He spreads photos of green English landscapes and contrasting cityscapes of grey buildings across the counter. "England would be best in the summer."

"I agree."

He side glances me. "I was waiting for the right person to go with."

"And going is on your bucket list," I remind him.

"Yeah, and that." He hops down from the stool and returns with a packet of chips. "I've noticed something strange, Phe."

"Stranger than us?" I take a chip and bite in half.

"About our lists. I was thinking about this again the other day. We can complete nearly all of the items in Australia."

"Because we live in an awesome country?" I reach for another chip.

"Do you think we're avoiding the rest of the world?"

"I just thought your list was deliberately local. I was surprised to see you're going overseas."

"Why?"

"The planning and... the time you have left."

"Oh, right." He rubs his head. "But you have no

excuse. There must be other countries you want to visit."

"There are."

"Then why aren't they on your list?"

"I don't know. I guess I could do those later."

Guy stiffens and for a few minutes falls silent. "So yours isn't really a bucket list, is it?"

"Yes!"

He shuffles the papers into a pile and pushes them back into the folder. "Did you write a list you thought we could do together and leave some items off that you want to do?"

"No. I'm just not brave enough to go far I guess." I sigh. "Don't start analysing things again, Guy. One minute you're teaching me to live in the moment and the next you're pulling things apart."

"Do you think we should change our lists?" he asks.

"Change them? You mean add things?"

"Put something challenging on the list, impossible to complete." The old intense Guy is back, a swing away from the carefree surfer at the beach. Strange that I'm more attracted to this Guy; that the energy he radiates at this time pulls me closer. I recognise the deep thoughts in his eyes, the emotion he submerges pushing upward. He's more of myself at times like this, and I consciously have to pull away.

"I think you'll find you have that on your list already, ghost hunting."

Guy raises a brow. "Don't you believe in an after-life, Ophelia?"

"I don't believe in ghosts."

"They haunt your dreams though, don't they?" He reaches across the counter and touches my hand.

I swallow hard. "No. They don't."

"They do. I've heard you in your sleep."

No. The nightmares live inside me; nobody hears and makes them reality. "Sorry if I woke you."

"I tried to wake you, but couldn't. You wouldn't let me hold you either." He pulls my hand to his lips and kisses me gently. "I wanted to wake you, tell you everything was okay."

"Thank you for caring."

"Of course I care. I worry though. I don't want you to be sick again."

I hop down from the stool and go to him, smooth his hair. "I'm fine. Better. Not the girl on the rocks."

The concern doesn't leave his furrowed brow. "But she hasn't disappeared completely. You have her under control, that's all. I don't want to be responsible for bringing her back again."

"You do the opposite, you know that," I whisper.

"I hope so. It was insensitive of me to think I could push you into overcoming your fears. Arrogant even." He slides an arm around my waist and holds me closer.

"Your mad yoga skills will help me recover," I say and wrap my arms around his neck. "Kiss me. I don't want to talk about this."

He does, slowly and tenderly, and then buries his face in my neck. Does he have the same fear for my future as I do?

"I think we need one impossible thing on our lists, that way we'll never finish them," he says and tightens his grip on my waist.

"Do you want to talk about what's happening to you?" I whisper into his hair.

"No. I can't."

"You never do, Guy. Sometimes I think talking might help you face what's happening. How are you right now?"

"You don't want to talk about you. I don't want to talk about me."

I move Guy's head, wishing I could dig my fingers inside and pull out what's killing him, and then hold his face so he has to look at me. "Just promise me you will if you need to. You can talk to me about anything. I'll do whatever I can to help."

Guy switches to what he does every time we touch on the subject of his death: he kisses me. The pattern has become predictable, as he pulls us from the edge and into life through the force of his passion. I can gauge the depth of his need to escape by whether his touch is rough and his lust uncontrolled, or whether he gently makes love to me. Either way, we push away the future threatening us and keep our heads above the water.

Guy lifts me onto the kitchen bench and presses himself between my thighs, hands wrapped in my hair as his mouth bruises mine. Desperate to join his attempt to throw us away from the direction our conversation headed, I grip his hips with my legs and match his intensity.

Sometimes when Guy's hands are on me, his skin against mine, I want to cry. Not because one day he'll never touch me again, but because he stirs in me something new. Guy's touch and kiss delves to the heart of who I am and frees the emotions I've hidden for years. We've spent days and nights exploring each other's bodies, in denial that with each moment we're together, we become more than lovers.

What we choose not to say is a louder denial than anything we do.

Guy rests his hands around my waist, holding me in place. His fingers bite into my skin, but I don't care, barely notice. Only when he stops kissing me do I realise my lips are swollen from the fierce passion of the last few minutes.

Guy drags a thumb across my mouth. The hidden is unguarded for a moment as our eyes meet in understanding.

"Are you okay?" I ask.

"I love you, Phe," he says, pushing damp hair

from my face.

His admission knocks down the foundations of the lies we've lived out, and the tears I promised I wouldn't cry over him sting my eyes. "I knew this couldn't stay simple."

The eyes searching mine aren't filled with tenderness but with confusion. "Why do I love you?" he asks, wiping my face with both hands. "Why did we do that?"

"I think sometimes love creeps up on you however hard you try and hide," I whisper and pull him closer. "I love –"

"No! Don't say it!" Guy's eyes widen in alarm.

"Why? I'm telling the truth. Look at us. Think about us." Our bodies remain joined in a way that feels so natural my heart hurts. Even though our skin touches, I'm aware of nothing but the strange energy that surrounds us when we're together.

"I know and I never thought I'd meet somebody like you. I never thought I'd fall in love. I didn't think it was possible."

Again, the words should be affectionate; but he's unhappy, as he grips me against him.

"Guy, can't we live in our moment as usual?" I whisper.

Guy moves his head and gently places kisses across my face, the warmth returning. "I'm okay to love you but please, don't love me," he murmurs.

He's not allowed to avoid this, to be in this on his own. "Too late. I love you. Who you are and how you make me feel. Now. Here. In this moment."

I gaze back into the dark blue water of his eyes, watch as the sadness lifts, and he relaxes. "I guess we fell under together," he says.

"I guess we did."

"Come here." Guy pulls me to him and I settle against his chest; his heart thuds against my ear. "I'm sorry."

"For what?"

"For whatever happens next."

"Us. We're what happens next," I whisper and hold him tighter.

The words are spoken, a line crossed greater than the one we stepped over when our relationship became sexual. This changes everything – and nothing because we've been in this place for months.

CHAPTER TWENTY-TWO

Erica sits cross-legged on my bed, as I prepare for our planned night out and picks up my phone.

"Holy crap, Phe. Is that Guy?" She turns the phone around; the wallpaper is a picture of Guy and me I took a couple of nights ago, on an evening walk through the park close to his house. He's pulling a goofy face, but even that doesn't detract from his looks; I chose this picture because the happiness I hope I cause shines in his eyes.

"Yes."

She shakes her head. "Whoa. Nice catch. No wonder you never showed me a picture before. How old is he?"

"Twenty-three."

Erica continues to stare. "He can't be a nice person, too. Guys who look like this are either arrogant or gay."

I laugh at her pigeonholing. "Sure, Erica. You might find him a bit intense or odd, but he's a great person. And definitely not gay!"

"He must be good. Your dark clouds have gone." Erica stands and heads over to where I'm painting my eyes with shimmering gold eye shadow. "I'm happy for you. Can't wait to meet him!" She nudges me. "So you chose him over Coffee Shop Guy?"

Ross. I worried about visiting the cafe following our cancelled date but he was laidback about the situation. He teased me about breaking his heart and I apologised profusely. In the end, Ross told me to stop being embarrassed every time I brought a coffee. I still visit daily, but I've never taken Guy to the place.

Erica's last visit to Perth was over two months ago, but those months feel like years. I chat to her regularly, gave her a condensed version of my relationship with Guy. I haven't told Erica about his illness, imagining the fuss she'll make over my involvement with him. Or maybe that's my subconscious telling me I should worry more. Erica knows the Phe I'm moving away from and I want her to meet the new, more confident one. Erica needs to see who I'm becoming, not worry about what will happen.

In the weeks since Guy's and my relationship switched gear, life has gathered pace. The trust that tentatively grew between us finally built a bridge between our lives. We have an unspoken rule that we hold our secrets within our relationship and don't share with anybody outside. Guy's right, now we've stepped into our world, it's hard to be back in theirs.

"I'm sure you'll like him." Depending on what mood he's in. Guy's quieter moods increased recently; he denies his behaviour is because of our admission, but I worry that the words were a step too far. Then he tempers this with the exuberant Guy, the one who tells me he loves me and the truth is plain in his eyes, so my fear dissipates.

"He must be special if you've fallen for him. I can see the change in you. Are you still seeing the psych regularly though?"

"I've learnt not to miss appointments. Besides, I have you nagging me if I do!"

"Yes, I'll come over here and haul your ass to the doctors if I ever think you need me to."

I set down my brush and pick up a pink lipstick, avoiding Erica's eyes. At my lowest, I never called her and if Erica knew, she'd be hurt. Yes, calling Erica would've made more sense than standing alone on the rocks, but she was busy and I didn't feel worth her time. I didn't feel worth anybody's time.

"Guy said he'll come along tonight," I say and rub some lipstick from the corner of my mouth.

"Does he have any hot friends he could bring?" she asks with a grin.

"What happened to Rob?"

"We finished things. We weren't much of a couple anymore; he hardly had time for me." Erica picks a pair of earrings from a jewellery box on the dresser.

"If you date a footballer, you've got to expect him to be busy in football season."

"That wasn't all he was busy with." Erica purses her lips, her nonchalance slipping.

"Oh. Another girl?" I ask, as if I need to.

"Yeah." She holds the silver strands against her ear. "Can I borrow these?"

Erica and Rob were the high school couple predicted to be the childhood sweethearts married and together for life. I'm surprised Erica didn't say anything. She's always there for me and it was my turn to be there for her.

"Sorry to hear that. Why didn't you say? And sure, borrow them."

"I'm honestly not bothered. We drifted months ago; a natural end. I guess by the time we finished we were friends more than anything."

"Right."

How can she be so blasé about her break-up? This and my resistance to filling her in on details about my life are new measures against how much is changing. The physical distance between Erica and me is matched by the fading friendship as our lives travel away from each other.

Erica steps back and admires her earrings. "I'm good. I'm happy. So are you, let's go!"

We head out to the local pub, where we've arranged to meet Guy. I assured Erica she won't be third wheel; Guy will stay for a drink and then leave. She was the one insisting on meeting him; Guy's busy and Erica's visit from Melbourne is too short-lived to organise anything but this brief catch up.

Seven p.m. and the pub is filled already, groups filling the round wooden tables as more joining them with loud hellos. I recognise some from regular Saturday night visits here with Jen and occasionally Guy. We head to the crowded bar and I squeeze between two groups while attempting to attract the barman's attention. Erica squashes next to me, and a few minutes later, drinks in hand, we vainly look around the pub for a seat.

Two men I vaguely know approach us and I exchange awkward hellos. Clearly we've forgotten each other's names. This switches quickly to the two men not so subtly hitting on us. To my dismay, Erica joins in, flirting with one and leaving me to edge away from the other.

Two guys alone, two girls alone. I can guess what they think's going to happen. Also, as often happens, one is better looking than the other, although neither is comparable to Guy. Andy, the taller and less attractive of the two with a crew cut and more muscles than I like in a man, keeps offering to buy me drinks and moves closer. I politely decline and pull my phone out of my bag to text my missing boyfriend. Thankfully, the music in the venue is loud ensuring conversation with Andy can be avoided.

"Is Guy not coming?" Erica says into my ear as she watches me.

"He should be here soon."

Guy hasn't responded to my text, asking where he is. He chose this meeting place; I don't understand why he hasn't appeared. Yesterday he laughed at my excitement of seeing Erica after a couple of months and told me he was looking forward to meeting her. So where is he?

"And did you ask if he was bringing any friends?"

I indicate the attentive guy next to her. "Does that matter now?"

She grins. "I guess not."

Increasingly pissed off with how close her beau's friend is moving toward me, I maintain focus on my phone and give polite smiles instead of speaking. Erica's out to enjoy herself, and I'm worried about Guy.

Following the third message, I finally receive a response. <I can't make it. Sorry>

<Are you okay?>

<I have to stay home tonight>

Is he unwell? He was fine yesterday. <Okay>

<Are you out?>

<Yes. Erica's having fun>

<Don't have too much fun without me>

<Are you sure you're alright?>

<Kind of>

Kind of? I glance at Erica, I can imagine the reaction if I drag her away from her new friends to Guy's place. She's complained about her lack of social life recently and is determined to enjoy her weekend away. This situation is reminiscent of the time I dropped everything when I arranged a date with Ross.

<What do you need? Are you sick?> I type

<Don't stress. Come over tomorrow?>

<I'll come over tonight if you need>

<No. Have fun with Erica. I'll be fine>

<I'll call when I get home>

<Sure thing. Night, beautiful girl xx >

I do stress. Guy pushes a lot beneath his surface and rarely admits he needs help, for him to hint he's not doing well is unusual. When I tell Erica that he isn't coming, she's disappointed momentarily then returns to her new friends. This irritates me; didn't Erica come to see me? This irritation spreads to an exchange of words over the 'random guys' situation. As Guy isn't coming, I persuade Erica to leave for somewhere she can dance. Somewhere away from these annoying men.

CHAPTER TWENTY-THREE

The next afternoon, I drop Erica at the airport and head over to Guy's place. His messages this morning were brighter, quelling my fear he's becoming sicker. I researched brain tumours again but stopped reading after a few minutes, feeling intrusive. The nagging voice telling me I'm doing the wrong thing becoming attached to Guy starts. *Becoming?* I am attached.

A dishevelled Guy answers the door, blinking at the sunshine. "What time is it?"

"Three. Are you okay?"

Dark circles rim his eyes and his hair sticks up, so I smooth a strand down. The front of his half-undone white shirt is covered with a rainbow of colour, like a smock used on children at kindergarten. Streaks of yellow run down his face.

"Three. Wow." He steps back. "Come on in."

Guy strides back into the house and immediately begins gathering up items from the dining table. A4 sheets of paper scrawled with drawings I can't make out, oil pastels spilled on the floor.

"Oh!" He drops the pile back down and seizes my face. "I never said hello."

I stumble as he slams his mouth against mine, taking advantage of my parted lip surprise as he delves his tongue into my mouth. I remain in frozen bewilderment, unable to respond so he lets my face go.

"Feeling better then?" I ask.

"I am." He rubs his thumb against my lip. "I'll tidy up and we'll go out."

"Where?"

"No idea!" He scrunches the papers back into his arms and pokes the pastels into a pile with his foot.

"Maybe you should change?"

"Good idea. I'll take a shower. Want to join me?"

"Umm."

"I'm sorry I got distracted last night," he says and opens a nearby cupboard, shoving the papers inside. I catch sight of more stacked inside.

"Erica wanted to meet you."

"Ah." He scrunches his nose. "Tonight?"

"She only stayed the weekend remember?"

"Is it Saturday?"

"No, Sunday."

He grins. "Whoops!"

"Whoops?"

"I missed a day. I thought you called Friday?"

"No." I sigh. "Have you slept, Guy?"

"I don't think so. I wasn't feeling too great, so I called you, and then spent time drawing instead. And painting. I guess I lost track of time."

"You said you weren't feeling well?" I clench my teeth. Last night was an excuse. He didn't want to meet my friend.

"I was fine, just not up to going out. There're people I don't particularly want to see."

"In Northbridge?"

"Every time I go into the city at night I see them, and they hassle me."

"Who?"

"People. Nobody important." He rubs his face with both hands, a shadow of concern on his face. "I hope

I didn't upset your friend."

No, but you upset me. "All good." I indicate the remaining mess on the wood floor. "Looks like you were very productive last night."

"Sure was! Right. Shower." He heads up the stairs, and then reappears seconds later. "Coming?"

"No."

"Damn shame!"

I perch on the sofa feeling as if drawn into a whirlwind and spat out again.

After ten minutes debating whether to open the cupboard and look at Guy's work, he reappears in fresh boardies and a t-shirt.

Guy shuffles across the sofa next to me. "We could stay home?" he suggests, trailing his fingers across my face. In response, as ever, my face and body flare with heat.

"You said you wanted to go out?"

"Mmm." Guy kisses my neck, lips remaining on my pulse point as his arm snakes around my waist. "I know, but I think I want to be alone with you."

When his other hand creeps up my thigh, I grab his fingers. "Guy! Why get ready to go out and then start this?"

His fresh scent pulls me further into memories of sex, the fruit of his shampoo and ocean fragrance of his soap reminding me how this tastes on his skin. Ignoring me, he plants kisses along my neck and collarbone, gripping my leg as he does. I shift against him, fighting the desire to do exactly what he's indicating.

Suddenly, he pulls away. "I did something else last night! I forgot to tell you."

He hops back off the sofa and I catch my breath, touching my skin where his lips were. Guy paces around the room, looking under magazines then walks into the kitchen. I've seen Guy focused and happy before, but this is odd. Does his brain tumour do this to him?

"I lost it." He stands in the kitchen doorway, lips pursed.

"What are you looking for?"

"Paper. A print out." He waves his hands around and scans the room.

"In there?" I suggest and point at the cupboard.

Guy smacks his forehead with the palm of his hand. "Of course!" He roots around inside and produces two pieces of paper. "Here. I got a copy for you."

Guy passes me a booking confirmation for flights to England in July. "Guy!"

"What?"

"You can't do this! I need to check if I can take the time off work. I told you that."

"Well, now you have the dates."

"I can't say yes!"

"Why? Phe, I need to go soon." He perches on the coffee table opposite me, shoulders slumping.

I reach out and touch his face. "Are you sure you're okay? You seem a bit... agitated."

"Do I? Sorry. I become too focused on things sometimes."

"Your love for life," I say with a smile.

"Making the most. Sometimes there aren't enough hours in the day so I make more." Guy picks at the yellow paint stuck beneath his nail.

"By not sleeping?"

"Occasionally." He points at the sheet. "Go on, take that, and give the date to HR at work. Say yes."

I look carefully at the flight times – and cost. "Have you paid for this?"

"Yes. I want to. Don't pay me back."

"I can't do that! That's your money!"

"Can't take all this with me, Phe." He rubs his nose with the back of his hand. "I thought maybe you could have my house too."

"Wow. Guy. Can we stick to one topic of

conversation?" And not that one.

"Fine. Take it." He points at the paper. "Book your holidays from work then we'll plan more of what to do."

I carefully fold the sheet and push the paper into my pocket. "Maybe you should rest, Guy. Settle a bit."

He scrunches his face. "Am I too much? There's so much I want to do before they... before I run out of time."

I stand. "How about I go home and you come over to mine later?"

His face dimples. "You mean when I've calmed down?"

"You're exhausting! I'm tired from last night. This was supposed to be a quick visit to see if you were alright."

"I am absolutely fine." He kisses me briefly on the mouth.

"If we're going out, I need to change too." I indicate my scruffy black track pants and loose grey top.

"No worries, I'll come over later. I guess I should have some breakfast."

"Lunch."

He grins. "Lunch."

Guy disappears into the kitchen leaving me with an uncertainty I can't place my finger on, and a certainty there's something going on with him he's choosing to hide.

CHAPTER TWENTY-FOUR

Guy appears at my house a couple of hours later, bringing with him energy I swear he shouldn't have. A thought strikes and I study him. Does Guy do drugs? If he's living life to the fullest and staying up all night, that could be how he manages.

"Are you okay?" he asks, searching my face in return.

"I am. Have you slept yet?"

"No. I wanted to see you." He slips his hand behind me and grabs my ass. "I was going to suggest we stay home, but I really want to go into the city."

"You do? Last night you didn't!" I bristle.

"I have something to show you, too! Hurry up!" He points at my handbag. "Got everything?"

"Yes."

"Let's go!"

When we head out of the house, Guy stops next to a black sports car I don't recognise. The lights flash as he hits the remote and I stare.

"You have a new car?"

"Yeah. Like it?"

"Very nice. Expensive."

Without replying, Guy climbs inside. I join him, perching onto the cool cream leather seat. The weird combination of new car scent mingles with Guy's familiar cologne.

A car isn't needed for the length of the journey we're taking; a bus would be as good. Strange that Guy wanted to flaunt this; recently he's chosen to drive his Jeep over his flashier cars. "You must have a lot of money," I say.

"You know I do. You're funny that you never ask why."

"I didn't think it was my business." I smooth my short dress. So many questions I haven't asked because I choose not to. "Where's your money from if you don't work?"

"I inherited a lot. My father was one of the original Silicon Valley millionaires. He was part of the team who invented the internet." He glances at me. "Impressive, huh?"

"I guess. Yes. He was American?" My scalp prickles, and the voice asking why I've chosen not to pry grows louder. "You're not American, are you?"

"No, Aussie. My mum was, and I was born here. My father died a last year ago and as the only surviving kid, I inherited all the money."

Another ignored question pushes up. "Right. So you have no family?"

"Not really. Not close by, anyway."

"Don't you feel isolated going through all this on your own?"

"I was always isolated, Phe," he says quietly. "Put some music on!"

The volume of the sound system assaults my ears as he hits a control and I grab at the dial in front of me. "Guy! Turn that down!"

"Sorry!" The music quiets and he gestures at the LCD screen listing radio stations. "Your choice."

I swallow down the feeling something definitely isn't right with Guy and choose the first station saved to his device. Has he had bad news about his condition and chosen to live harder and faster?

****

The club Guy chooses is on the outskirts of the popular areas; and immediately, I'm on edge. The clientele are a world away from the club I spent the night in with Erica last night. Opening straight onto the street, steps lead down from the unmanned entrance and into a dim room. I adjust my eyes and hover at the edge of the doorway, against dark painted walls covered in classic movie posters and badly printed flyers for local bands. A tall man with a ponytail stands at the bar. With him is a girl in jeans and a black t-shirt with the sleeves roughly cut away. She looks at me with disdain. I thought I was going somewhere me and Guy usually visit and chose a dress I bought last week – light pink and feminine. Nobody else in this venue is light pink and feminine.

Guy doesn't speak to anybody, which confuses me further. If he's going to bring me somewhere like this, I'd presume he knew people. Even for a Sunday, the small room is filled.

I sit with Guy at the bar on a tall stool beneath the neon lights. "Why have we come here?" I ask.

"Because I don't want anybody to know I'm in the city," he says without looking at me, and raises his hand to call over the bar man.

I ask for a Coke and Guy laughs, then buys me one with vodka in. I'm not a big drinker; and since the disastrous night in Dunsborough, I haven't seen Guy drink much. Tonight he lines up shots, encouraging me to join in. I take one but retch at the sour tasting tequila.

"Get me another vodka instead," I whisper in his ear over the music. "With Coke, Guy."

"Ah." I watch as Guy calls the barman back over, and taps his wallet on the bar. The edginess remains, but his eyes are bright.

The scruffy barman looks at me with disinterest, as he places a glass on the bar in front of me, and several more shots in front of Guy.

I sit on the stool, tense, wanting nothing but to leave. How can I persuade Guy to go home before he gets wasted? Guy chatters exuberantly, as he does sometimes, talking about his plans for England. I attempt to interrupt a couple of times with my own suggestions, but he talks over me. I look into his eyes, and they're distant, as if he's recounting a film he's watching in his mind. Normally on days like these, I love his gregariousness and the light this brings to my life; but this evening he worries me.

"Are you sure everything is alright?" I ask Guy, witnessing his tenth shot.

"Yes!"

"You don't seem yourself."

"Phe! I'm just having fun! What's wrong with that?" He leans from his stool so his mouth meets mine, a hard, sudden kiss before he turns back and downs another shot with a wink at me.

"Some of us have to work tomorrow!" I protest.

"Ah, crap, sorry." He slides a hand along my leg, fingers disappearing under my dress. "Staying with me tonight?"

"I don't know. You're freaking me out a bit."

"Why?"

"You're intense today."

Guy holds both his hands up, palms out. "I'll stop. No more drinks."

"I think I want to leave." I climb down from the high barstool.

He runs a hand through his hair and watches me, remaining seated. "Some days, I want to forget."

I sigh and put a hand on his leg. "I understand that, but this isn't like you. I thought you went for natural highs."

Guy climbs down from the stool. "Do you think I'm high?" he asks, tugged brow showing disbelief.

"I don't know, are you?"

"No, I'm not. I don't do drugs anymore."

"Anymore?"

"Come on, everybody smoked a bit of weed when they were a teen. That's all I mean."

"I didn't!"

He snorts. "Fine. Well, nothing illegal. Promise."

I eye the line of empty shot glasses. "I don't think you can drive home."

"No worries, you can." He pulls his keys from a pocket and tosses them to me.

I catch them. I haven't had much to drink, but I'm not keen on driving his car. "Can we call a taxi?"

"Phe! Come on, I'm not leaving that car in the city overnight. It won't be there when I come back tomorrow." He grabs my hand. "Let's go back to mine."

I'm dubious about driving; I'm unused to cars this powerful. I attempt to drive and Guy giggles drunkenly at my second tyre screech in as many minutes until I get a handle on the car's performance and drive us to his house.

"We should go somewhere next weekend," he announces as I navigate the street through his suburb.

"Something on the bucket list?"

"Nope. Had enough of that for now."

But that's what we are. Who we are. Take that from the equation and we lose the one excuse that we're not one hundred percent a real couple. "What do you mean?"

"This."

"This?"

I wait for a reply; but Guy's now flicking through the radio stations, the jarring of each track change confusing me. "Turn the music down."

He does. Then says nothing. With the amount of alcohol Guy's had, I'm surprised the journey hasn't lulled him to sleep.

We arrive and head into his darkened house. Guy strides ahead, flicking switches until every downstairs room is brightly lit. I follow him into the kitchen, squinting.

The paper and pastels are back, strewn across the table; the kitchen sink filled with empty mugs and glasses. "Drink?" he asks, taking a couple of glasses from the glass-fronted cupboard.

"No." He pulls a bottle of wine from the rack anyway. "Can you stop now, please?"

For a few moments, he watches me. "Okay. Something else?"

Before I register what's happening, the kitchen door slams closed behind me and I'm pinned against the wood, my head held firmly by Guy as his mouth crashes onto mine. My mind protests but my body yields immediately, the need in his kiss snatching my breath. Guy lifts me against his hips, hand sliding under my ass beneath my dress, and digs his fingers into the skin. I pull my mouth away and Guy moves to my neck nipping along the soft skin until he reaches my collarbone. Pinioning me, he pulls my dress away from my shoulder, the material straining as the straps are stretched downwards.

Nothing is said, he doesn't look at me, then focuses on his exploration of my exposed breasts, his breath speeding. Do I stop him or go with the moment? Guy shifts my weight then drags my panties to one side, and I take a sharp intake of breath as he thrusts a finger into me. He murmurs something against my skin and slides a second finger in, pushing his thumb onto my clit at the same time.

I'm stunned, but don't stop him. This is the first time he's physically connected with me in days, and I crave being wanted by him. I don't want to stop. Guy's passionate, but never unrestrained like this. The movement of his hand sparks a lust of my own and I drag his head to mine, and push my tongue into his mouth.

He withdraws his fingers, grabs me under the ass again, and presses me into the wall. "Jesus, I've wanted to fuck you all night," he breathes and sinks his teeth into my shoulder.

I inhale sharply at his words and action. Guy's breath comes in hard, fast pants against my neck as he returns to pressing his fingers inside me, sucking on my nipples. I didn't expect this to turn me on so readily, but the intensity of the evening spills over and I'm lost to him.

Guy struggles with the button on his jeans, and I help unzip him. He drops me to the floor for a moment and pulls a condom from his back pocket.

"I would take you to bed, but I want to do this here," he says in a low voice.

My heart hammers against my chest. The intensity rolling from him isn't frightening, but contagious, being desired on this level, looked at as if he wants to devour me delves to the centre of my primal self too.

"Here?" I ask hoarsely. I fix my eyes on his, hear him open the wrapper and slide the condom onto himself.

"Fuck, yes." Guy pulls me up against the wall again, and the tip of him pushes against me. He pauses long enough for me to indicate if I've changed my mind, but I hold his waist and pull him closer.

Green light given, Guy thrusts into me and I catch my breath. One arm on the wall above me, and the other gripping my backside, Guy continues to push, watching my expression. I shift against him, matching his shallow breaths as my body slams against the wood of the door. Guy grabs the back of my thighs and pulls my legs apart, rocking into and stretching me. I grab a handful of his hair and pull his face up, grazing my teeth against his lip. He growls and pushes harder, more frenzied than he's ever been.

"You're so tight," he gasps and plunges his tongue into my mouth again.

One of my shoes falls, hitting the floor. The other follows but I barely notice anything but the building orgasm. I hold my breath against the wave, tightening around Guy until the shattering bliss hits. I bite into his shoulder to stop crying out; and within seconds, Guy matches my release, pushing himself to the hilt.

For a moment, he rocks against me and my awareness of my surroundings returns, the hard wood against my back and the awkward position Guy's holding me at. He gently releases me and steadies me as I stumble to my feet.

"That was intense," he murmurs and covers my face with kisses.

I hold onto him. "You're telling me! What the hell has got into you?"

Guy removes the condom and ties a knot before slinging it into the kitchen bin and I adjust my clothes.

"Living life with the girl I love," he says as he returns, zipping up his jeans. His face is flushed, perspiration across his forehead as he looks at me with eyes filled with painful tenderness.

"Are you really okay?" I whisper and touch his mouth.

"Yes. Stop worrying." He slaps my ass. "Bed. More where that came from."

I step back and cross my arms. "What if I don't want to spend the night with a sex-crazed man?"

He grins. "But that's the exact reason you should want to stay here tonight."

Guy takes my hand and kisses my fingers in a romantic gesture that's strange considering the animalistic passion of several minutes ago. My legs shake from the hard, fast sex as we head upstairs. I don't know what should bother me more – Guy's behaviour or the fact I enjoyed what he did. Every day with Guy I take another step toward being a different person.

His.

CHAPTER TWENTY-FIVE

I spend the next day in a happy haze, body buzzing with the after effects of the night with Guy. Following the lust-filled encounter in the kitchen, he switched to lovemaking with an intense gentleness where he told me he loved me, and looked at me as if I was the most precious thing in the world.

Memories and images switch from making me blush to creating a need for more, but unease underlies the evening. Guy seemed calmer this morning, although he was already awake and working on his laptop when I woke. I can't shake the niggling worry that something has happened in his life to trigger the behaviour. With that, comes the fear over what – and why he hasn't told me.

I exchange a couple of texts with Guy and we arrange for him to come over to my place; I offer to cook. To my relief, Jen heads out for the evening with Cam and I shower and change.

The Guy who arrives a few hours later immediately worries me, carrying the air he does when things are troubling him. His eyes are sunken, the over-exertion of the last few days catching up on his pale face, ageing him.

"I need to talk to you," he says quietly as soon as I close the door.

"Alright..." *No kiss. No touch. Nothing.* A creeping anxiety replaces the happy buzz of the day. Guy glances at me then looks away. "Now?"

"I guess."

I head to the kitchen; but when I turn to speak to Guy, he's still in the hallway. His agitation is clear as he runs a hand across his hair, staring at his feet. I swallow; my sixth sense is correct and I don't want to be right.

"Everything okay?"

"Not really." He rests against the wall in the hallway.

"What's wrong, Guy? Has something happened?" I pause. "Did the doctor tell you something bad? Is that what's happening?"

He's retreated again, the way Guy folds inward, the peace and happiness lost. The other man, drowning. "This isn't good. This is wrong."

"What?"

In his eyes is a different person, not the one who looked at me tenderly and shared his heart. He's distracted, switched off, as if he sees through me. "I hurt people. I kill people."

"Guy, we spoke about this. What's happened?"

"They know and they told me this is wrong, that I shouldn't do this."

"Who knows?"

"My family. I knew they were watching me again. They're supposed to leave me alone, but they always interfere."

"Come and sit down."

Guy shakes his head and crosses his arms over his chest. "I should go."

"No. Don't!" I approach and take his arm, curling my fingers around his jacket. "Don't go. Explain to me about your family."

"Explain? Right. Because of what I did to my mum and sister, my father didn't want me. He sent me to live with my grandparents for years." Guy glances up at me. "Same as you, huh?" I nod. "My dad died a year ago – for once, not my fault – and I inherited a lot of money. I moved away from the others but that doesn't stop them following everything I do."

"Maybe they're worried about you and they want to mend bridges before you go?"

Guy digs his nails into his palms. "They don't care, they get into my head and tell me what to do. If I won't listen, they hassle me with reminders. Tell me how bad I am. Now they know about you and tell me to leave you alone."

"This is your life, Guy. Ignore them. We can decide what to do. So bad things happened in the past, make this good. You won't hurt me."

"That's the problem! One day, I will!" He runs both hands down his face. "I thought maybe this time I wouldn't, that something good would survive."

"What do you mean? Guy, please." As he places a hand on the door handle, I step forward in alarm. He can't leave like this, with misunderstandings. "Tell me. Tell me what's wrong, you need to."

He places his hands on the door, facing away from me. His rapid breathing and stiff stance are unlike anything I've seen from Guy before. "I haven't just killed my mother!" he says through clenched teeth. "I don't just hurt those I love. People die around me. My sister – killed her. My girlfriend – killed her."

I step back and cross my arms, eyes widening. "What?"

He turns back to me and looks down. "So yeah, maybe your housemate is right. I am a psycho!"

For the first time, I'm scared of Guy. His height and bulk threaten me, and I know his strength. Then I look into his deep blue eyes and all I see is pain. He's not a threat. On the beach when he told me about his mother, that was his interpretation and not reality. "Killed them or they died?"

"Died because of my actions. What if you do?" I attempt to take hold of him again and he throws my hands off his arms. "No. I'll kill you, too."

"Guy, calm down."

"Don't you see? I let myself fall into this, thought you could save me, but all I'll do is take you down with me." The agitation on his face spreads to his body as he drags his hands repeatedly through his hair. "Shit, shit, shit. See, we shouldn't have gone there. We should've stopped."

A key turns in the lock and Guy jumps away from the door. A surprised Jen walks into the house. The relaxed smile on her face freezes when she sees Guy.

"Are you okay?" she asks me.

"Fine."

"You don't look fine. What's happening?"

Guy pushes past her and out of the house. Jen stumbles then stares after him. "Jesus, that man is rude."

I hang onto the pain spreading across my chest from where he tore the piece of himself away I thought he'd given, and give Jen a false smile.

"Sorry, we had a row. All good."

Jen shakes her head. "He's bad news, Phe. I keep telling you. Don't get messed up by him."

She heads into the house and I stand in the doorway, hand on the door. Do I follow him? Closing the door behind, I head down the low stone steps and along the path. The road is busy with cars and people strolling along the pavement in the autumn sunshine, living their ordinary lives. No Guy. Unable to know which direction he went, shaken by the encounter, I step away.

Guy took hold of me and shoved me hard, backwards. I don't allow myself close to people because I can't open up, frightened they won't understand what lies beneath my facade.

Look what happens the first time I let somebody into my world.

CHAPTER TWENTY-SIX

Guy doesn't answer my calls or texts. Nothing. Ordinarily, I'd take this as meaning something is over; if a friend stops replying, I take the hint. In my limited experience with men, this is clearly 'leave me alone'.

But my sixth sense won't let me. This is a man, whose mask slipped and revealed somebody torn by pain, lashing out to push me away. This is the man who I'm starting to care deeply for, and he's drowning.

Two days later, unable to stop thinking and worrying, I push away my pride and head to Guy's house. Maybe he's embarrassed, and doesn't know how to contact me.

Maybe he doesn't want to.

A woman answers the door, and the surprise on her face matches mine. Worry etches her delicate features, but all I notice is how stunning she is. Tall, graceful with dark auburn hair tied back, accentuating her sculpted face. She looks a few years older than me, but not much.

"Um. I'm Phe. I'm wondering..." I trail off as she scrutinises me. "I'm looking for Guy."

The lady's hand rests on the door, a large diamond ring above a wedding band. *Oh, God, please, no.* "Guy?"

"Guy Drew. He lives here."

She frowns. "You know Noah?"

"Noah?"

"Noah. The man who lives here."

The locked gate holding back all the minor suspicions I've held about him is unlocked by her words and the hidden doubts rush out.

"He said his name was Guy," I say and hate how pathetic and stupid that sounds.

The woman steps back and opens the door wider. "He is Guy, but he's Noah too."

"Are you his..." I wave my hand at her rings. "Am I a complete idiot?"

She smiles. "I'm Lottie. Noah's cousin."

Noah. What the hell is going on?

"So he's not here?"

"Are you involved with him?"

Her quaint expression confuses me further. "We're friends. More than. It's complicated. I was worried about him, we had an argument a couple of days ago, and I haven't heard from him since."

"He's not here, Noah's back in hospital and I've come to collect some of his things."

"Oh. Right."

"He has told you he's ill, hasn't he?" I nod, and she watches me warily. "He doesn't like to see people when he's in hospital. If you like, I'll ask if he wants to see you."

"He'd phone if he wanted to see me," I say defeated. He could've called me. I'd have helped. "He will be back out of hospital again, won't he?"

"Yes, but I'm not sure how long until he is. I'll tell Noah you were looking for him."

"No, it's fine. Probably best leave things."

"I hope you don't think I'm rude, but I'm inclined to agree with you."

Yes, rude, but I fix on a smile I don't feel like giving.

That evening the encounter cycles around in my head, and

I convince myself Lottie lied. Then I conclude I've been lying to myself. By the end of the evening, I've come to the conclusion Guy is married to Lottie and they both lied to me: about his name, his situation, and who he is. The hospital is the missing link. If this is the one truth, other parts could be too. But if Guy doesn't want to see me, what difference does the truth make?

CHAPTER TWENTY-SEVEN

"I'm kinda glad he's gone," says Jen.

Her out of the blue comment surprises me, interrupting my half-hearted viewing of the news as we sit together in our lounge room. "Guy?"

"Yeah. Something about him was off."

"I expect so, since he's dying." I look at my phone for the tenth time in as many minutes, waiting for a response from Erica.

Jen's silence doesn't last long. "He looked fine to me."

"Doesn't mean he is."

No message.

"So where is he?"

"In hospital?"

"Where?"

"I don't know."

"He didn't say?"

I look at Jen with an expression that tells her to shut up. "No. I haven't seen him since that night two weeks ago. Like you said, he's gone."

The seed of doubt planted by Lottie germinates. Guy lied about his name. What else?

"Phe, I think you have a romantic notion about Guy that stops you seeing the truth."

"What truth?"

Jen cradles her mug of coffee and sips. "You haven't told me much about him and I understand why, because I don't like him. How did you meet?"

"Weird story."

She sighs. "Right. Do you know his friends?"

"Some of them. He's a bit of a loner."

"And what's wrong with him?"

"Brain tumour."

"Hmm." Jen drains the rest of her coffee. "Tell me, if he cares about your relationship, why would he go to hospital and not tell you where?"

"I told you, we had an argument and maybe he was too sick to tell me."

"Two weeks ago. And he hasn't been in touch? No, Phe. Get out, now."

"I care about him," I whisper.

"He obviously doesn't care about you."

I don't hear anything else Jen says to me, her words echo the voice in my head telling me the same, but the one in my head goes further. He told you he loved you and lied. Don't trust him.

But I allowed myself to love him; to open my heart to a man I knew would leave me eventually.

Although I never expected us to end like this.

CHAPTER TWENTY-EIGHT

The work pressure lessened when I spent time with Guy, pushing that side of my life into a compartment instead of being my focus. Now Guy's disappeared, I'm aware that our relationship was my new focus. Instead of obsessing about every word I wrote at work, I'd obsess about everything I did with Guy.

I'd swapped using one thing to try to complete me to another. The fear of failure followed me, as with everything else in my life; but the idea I've been fooled beyond anything I could've predicted drags me down. After my third late night phone call in as many days seeking solace from the gathering clouds, Erica insists I return to the doctors. I'm angry, not only with Guy; but at how easily I can slip back toward the depression. The insidious darkness isn't the worst, but the fear. Fear this will always control me.

My psychiatrist refuses to touch my medication until I've spoken to a psychologist again. This is a typical pattern too, a visit to a psychologist equals somebody attempting to tell me my thinking is all wrong. They don't understand it's easier to protect myself than open up. Unless I unlock the padlock to the chain that's dragging me under I won't move on.

Guy's right. I'm terrified of life and I'm hiding.

But look what happened when I put my trust into somebody who could show me life wasn't the way I thought. He lied.

I leave an initial meeting with the psychologist where I attempted to field attempts to talk about my past, and head out to the grounds of the hospital where the clinic is located. As I have twenty minutes until my bus arrives, I check work emails and wander through the leafy grounds. I smile at the message from Erica on screen wishing me good luck but the smile freezes when there's one from Guy underneath.

<Phe. Sorry. Can explain.>

The emotions of the last four weeks hit with a deluge and I sink onto a low wall next to the clinic entrance. Cars pass by, circling and searching for parking spaces as I stare at the name. Guy. *Not Guy.* My first instinct is to ignore him, bury him back under, but my anger takes over.

<Noah. I don't want to see you.>

The cool autumn breeze picks at the edge of my skirt as I remain seated, phone in hand, debating what to do. My head hurts after the session with the psych, as exhausted as if I'd run a marathon and Guy's contact pushes me further to hiding back in my house.

<I need to explain>

<Like lying about your real name?>

<No. Phe. Please>

<I don't want to see you unless you explain everything. Who you are and why you're sick. If you are sick and didn't lie about that too.>

My stomach fills with acid as I stare at the words I want to yell at him instead reduced to letters on a phone screen. How do they sound in his head when he reads them? Does he hear anger? Hurt?

<I will explain> he replies.

I expected silence or a ducking away from the topic, not an agreement. The world around retreats as I'm locked into the conversation on my phone screen, mind tumbling with questions I want to ask.

<Where are you?> I ask.

<Home. Where are you?>

<Clinic. Psych>

<Are you okay?>

<What do you think?>

<Tell me where you are and I'll come for you.>

I tip my head to the blue Perth sky, the one that stretches forever, rarely cloudy. How can I trust him?

****

I refuse Guy's offer and take a taxi to his house. He offered to come to mine instead, but this is on my terms. I want his explanation and then I can draw a line. Move on. When I arrive, a shirtless Guy opens the door. If I weren't so angry, I'd be distracted by the memory of his body against mine. His dark denim jeans mould his lithe figure but his eyes are again circled by dark shadows, blond hair grown longer and mussed.

"Hello, Phe," he says, voice soft.

Colour covers the fingertips of his hand resting on the door, a rainbow from the pictures he never shows me. I don't respond and he opens the door wider so I can walk inside.

The house is as pristine as ever, and I follow him into his large lounge. We stand awkwardly and I cross my arms over my chest in case he attempts to hug me. Guy grabs a grey t-shirt with a faded logo and drags it over his head.

"Who are you?" I demand. "Why did your cousin say you were Noah? Why did you lie about your name?"

"I *am* Guy." He drags a wallet from his back pocket and flicks open before pulling out his driver's licence. "Noah is my first name, but I don't use it anymore."

I stare at the licence. Noah Guy Drew. "Anymore?"

"I didn't lie. My family calls me Noah still, but Guy means nothing to them." We stand close but further apart than we've ever been.

"The name or the person means nothing?"

"Both. When I moved to Perth last year, I left everything behind that I could. I couldn't have them controlling me anymore. I think being around them caused me to do the bad things."

"What bad things? You keep mentioning them, but never explaining properly."

"My mother, my sister... other people. If I stay away, I can't cause any problems."

I cross my arms tighter, and keep my distance. "But don't they care you're dying? Don't they want to help you?"

"Lottie does, she understands and I can ask her for help." He smiles. "She checks up on me anyway. Takes me to the hospital if things go downhill. I don't mind when she's in my head."

The room is empty of photographs or signs of life. Even show homes have fake pictures of smiling people, taken from the stock photo sites I spend time combing at work. Why did I never notice?

Wrong.

I noticed a lot, but never allowed myself to pay attention.

One thing has changed in the room. A huge canvas artwork spans the previously bare lounge wall. An ocean landscape, dark blue, the sky powdered by rainbows reflecting on the water like an oil slick. Drawn in by the vibrancy, I walk over until the picture encompasses my vision.

"That's you," Guy says from behind me. "And me."

Despite the vivid combination of primary colours,

the rainbow sky holds a chaos at odds with the still water. The dark ocean looks safer, somehow. I turn back to Guy and stare at his coloured fingers.

"What do you mean?"

"When I look at you, I see a girl who's a world away from the one who almost took her own life. But I also see she's hovering around you again. The colour radiating from you recently is fading. I wanted to capture my memory of you. Us. You're hurting, and it's my fault."

"I'm not hurt. I'm angry with you," I lie.

"I understand. I disappeared, never got in touch and —"

"No, that isn't why." What I denied when we were together can't be ignored anymore. Why was I willing to look naïve and stupid when I figured this out long ago?

Sometimes, believing the lies we tell ourselves is easier than dealing with the truth.

"You're not sick, are you Guy? Not physically. You've lied."

Guy drags his fingers through his hair and leaves his hands enmeshed, elbows sideways out as he gazes back at me. "I *am* unwell."

"*Have* you lied to me? Are you dying?"

Guy closes his eyes. "I am."

"What's wrong with you?"

In a sudden movement, Guy crosses to a tall beech-coloured unit and pulls open a drawer at the bottom. He scrabbles around inside and drags out a sheet of paper. His bucket list. Guy thrusts the paper at me; extra items are scrawled out from last time he showed me.

"I have to finish this, but I don't want to anymore."

I don't take the paper. "Why?"

"Because when I do, I'm going to die." His flat tone is one of acceptance, of somebody who's given up and won't fight anymore. For the first time since I stepped into the house, my heart twinges pain.

"How? How can you pinpoint that?"

Guy grips the paper in his hand then slowly sits on the large leather sofa nearby. "Do you believe in euthanasia?"

His words sting. "Are you talking about yourself? Are you in pain?"

"Always. Until I met you. Now I'm too scared to finish my list. I promised myself that's what I'd do, before I killed anybody else."

"You're making no sense. Promised you'd do what?"

In the following silence, the wave of truth builds, rolling forward ready to sweep us apart. "I don't deserve to have a life when they don't! How many more can I take? What if I take yours?"

"Guy, stop it!"

Breathing heavily, he scrunches the paper and stares at me. "When I've finished the last item, I'm going to end my life."

"Because you're in pain?" I ask, fighting the wave cresting above. "Because you don't want to suffer?"

"Because I'm not fucking worth it!" he shouts. "Haven't you listened? I don't deserve a life!"

The colour surrounding my vision melds, as the realisation hits and I'm pulled under. Deep down, I knew Guy hid the truth, but I never expected this. I can hardly form the words. "You're going to kill yourself?"

"Yes."

"Why?"

"I don't deserve to live."

I drag the words together as I fight for enough breath to speak. "Who told you that?"

"They do." He pushes his fingers against the side of his head. "Remember I believe in ghosts? Memories can be ghosts too, you know that. They push me to the edge, torture me, and I promised them – myself – I'd end everything before I destroyed anything else I loved."

An image of myself in the dusk on the edge of the rocks jumps into my mind. "No! You stopped me! You don't agree with running from life!" He doesn't respond. "You're lying! Saying this to make me leave! Can't you end our relationship like a normal person?"

"I *am* sick. The times I said I was in hospital I was, with people claiming they can save my life and make me better. I have a death sentence, Phe, people with my condition die all the time."

"What condition?"

Guy leaves the room, heading into the kitchen. He opens a cupboard and drags out white boxes with prescription labels attached. "When I was a teenager, they thought I was schizophrenic. Then they decided no, I was bipolar. Now they say I've got two for the price of one! But what the fuck does it matter what label they give me?" He slams the packets on the table in front of me. "I take all this and still the crap happens to people around me. Every time life goes okay, everything turns to shit again and somebody gets hurt. The things that happen to and around me aren't because I'm mentally ill. This is something I do! I'm not living the rest of my life in fear."

"Fear of what?"

Guy's stance and tone prickle the back of my neck. Is he dangerous? Is Guy saying he's going to hurt me? I grip my handbag, ensuring I'm close to the door.

"Aren't you listening?" he shouts. "Bad enough I can't have a normal life, but there're things controlling me. The doctors say they can control them, but the forces are bigger than that!"

The man in front of me maintains his sense of defeat, slumped against the kitchen counter as he looks at the floor with a down-turned mouth. Guy believes what he's saying, but his lucidity isn't matched by his sick rationality.

"Guy. I don't think you're well still."

"Of course I'm fucking not!"

"No, I mean you should be in hospital. Do you want me to call your cousin?" I ask gently.

"No point."

"There is! You can get better!"

"Bullshit, Phe!" he snaps his head up.

I take a deep breath. "You let me fall in love with you even though you were planning this?"

"I did something worse than that," he says hoarsely, moving toward me. "I fell in love with you."

I back away. "You're lying! You don't love me! Otherwise, you wouldn't stand there and tell me you want to kill yourself!"

"I don't want to, but I have to!"

"Why?" I shout back.

"So I don't hurt you!" He steps closer and reaches out before hesitating and lowering his hands.

"How mad does that sound, Guy? Can you understand how hurtful this is? The man who's spent months showing me how to live my life wants to fill it with unhappiness again by choosing to die. You're a fucking hypocrite!"

Guy's eyes widen. "Swearing. That's new."

"Don't fucking tease me!" I yell and push his chest. "You don't say things like this and then joke around!"

"I'm not." He seizes my arms. "Phe, I'm confused."

"*You're* confused? The man I love just told me his life isn't worth living, a life I thought I was part of."

"That's the issue." He drags me closer by the arms, short rapid breaths matching mine. "I've found somebody who makes life worth living."

"But you want to kill yourself! Let me go!"

"Let me explain."

I grab the list scrunched in his hand and stare through blurring eyes. His tenth item is scrawled out. 'Fall in love'. "Why did you cross that one off?"

"I told you. I love you."

I screw the list in my hand as I attempt to control my anger. "No! You don't! You're ill." My heart pounds, a black sickness overcoming me. "How could you do this knowing my history?"

"Phe. I don't want to anymore. I never want to finish my list!" He curls a hand around mine and grips, but I yank my fingers away.

"I can't trust you. Months and you didn't breathe a word. Lied, told me you had a brain tumour."

"I do have something in here!" He taps his head. "Pushing out my life. My illness may as well be a tumour. Nothing can cut this out of my head."

"I don't want to listen to any more of this craziness! I should never have let you into my life!" Mouth dry and heart pounding so hard that Guy's words fade into the background, I move into the hallway and to his front door.

"Don't leave!"

I pause and look back. "Please don't contact me again."

"Phe! I'm trying to explain to you why things are different now!"

A man covered in colour is the darkest I've seen him the whole time we've been together. Lost, confused, unhappy; but I'm numb from his words, desperately holding back from breaking down because I'm unsure if anger will be the first and unhelpful reaction. My hands shake and I tuck them beneath my arms.

"Things are very different now," I say hoarsely. "You're right."

"Please, don't leave, Phe," he says, standing in the kitchen doorway, shoulders slumped. "Don't let me destroy you too."

"You haven't destroyed me! I won't let you! So don't you dare add me to your deranged list of things you deserve to die for!" I snap.

Guy blinks several times. *Oh, my God, he believes he has.* "Okay."

"I'm a stronger person since I met you!" I jab myself in the chest. "Yes, you've torn away something that I believed in, that made me happy, but you're not tearing down who I am!" My heart twists with more pain than I'm willing to show. How can this man be the one I've held in there? "You need help. I can't help you."

"I can change. I am changing, just like you are."

"No! I don't even know you, Guy or Noah or whoever the hell you are!"

I startle as Guy's doorbell rings and he shoves his hands in his pockets, backing up. The shrill sound of Guy's ringtone interrupts me and he pulls his phone from his pocket. "Lottie." He listens for a few moments, staring at the floor. "Yes, I am at home." I faintly hear her voice from the phone. "I know. I'm fine now. I needed to speak to Phe."

Somebody bangs on the door. I turn and open it. Lottie looks in surprise at me, phone to her ear then ends the call and tucks the phone in her bag as she steps past.

"I said I'm fine! I'm not leaving with you again!" says Guy, turning back to the kitchen. "The hospital wouldn't have let me leave if they didn't think I'm okay!" he calls back.

Lottie rubs her eyebrow with delicate fingers as she turns her dark green eyes to me. "I thought you must be Phe. He mentioned you, and I put two and two together."

"Will he be alright?" I ask indicating the direction he headed.

"He's not dangerous, not to himself or others, despite what he thinks." She gently closes the front door. "He's back on his medication and heading in the right direction, maybe it's a good thing he saw you today, to explain. Although, I was trying to persuade him not to."

"Why?" I frown at her interference.

"In case you weren't coping, the last thing he needs is an hysterical ex."

I swallow. *Ex.* "Well, as you can see I'm not. He just told me his plans though. About wanting to kill himself."

"At least he's told people now." She rests against the wall and glances in Guy's direction.

"I really didn't know him, did I?" I whisper.

"He's not a bad person. Noah's experienced a lot of tragedy in his life, but I'm sure he can get through. He's stronger than he thinks."

An echo of Guy telling me the same runs across my mind. "I hope so. He seems good just… Unwell."

"Yes. I'm hoping now he's seen you he can accept that he hasn't repeated the past."

"What do you mean?"

Lottie chews her lip as she studies me. "Maybe one day he'll tell you about that himself."

"I don't think so. I can't see him again." I push down the Phe who wants to walk after Guy, take hold of him, and pull him from the edge the way he helped me. She's resurfacing from where I've submerged her in the confused, angry sadness of the last few weeks.

I came here expecting him to tell me where he'd been and why he'd lied, but this is beyond comprehension. "I have to go. Tell Guy – Noah – I hope things work out. I can't face him right now."

I pull open the door and step out of Guy's life. The cool air hits me, filling my lungs as I gasp in air. On the verge of a panic attack, I close my eyes and focus on slow, deep breaths.

Leave.

Guilt follows me to the bus stop, and I'm angry that the emotion even gets a look in. Why do I feel guilty when Guy's the one that caused the damage? If he had disappeared and never contacted me again, things would be easier than to find out he'd betrayed me so spectacularly. On the bus, I stare out of the window, lost at the edge of the deep water again, listening to the inhale and exhale of my breath.

In the last week, I'd moved away from him, accepted I wouldn't see Guy again; and now he emerges again and does this. My mind anaesthetised by the shock, I watch the world travelling past the window. But in my mind's eye is Guy and the anguish on his face when he spoke about his illness, when he told me how hurting me, hurt him.

I don't have the capacity to help somebody who deceived me for so long.

CHAPTER TWENTY-NINE

The days that follow Guy's confession pass in a deadened haze. I spend the time carefully picking at the painful cord wrapped around my heart, furious with myself for feeling how I do. I swore I wouldn't fall in love because the fallout would blow my life to pieces again, but I did. Yet, I surprise myself. With the aching emptiness comes the acceptance that this is not my fault. I did nothing wrong apart from tangle myself with a deceitful person. A sick mind. With my history, I'm aware how mental illness can create behaviour which well people would never consider, but I never dragged anybody down with me.

I understand little about the condition Guy told me about and I look at support sites. My heart tore again as I read other sufferers' stories, of their lifelong battle. This doesn't change my mind about Guy. He knew we were growing close, was aware I'd discover the truth eventually, but he didn't stop. Did Guy intend to carry out his plans? That one thought alone sickens and confuses me the most.

Who did I fall in love with? Guy. A man who doesn't exist.

Over the next couple of weeks, Guy attempts to call, his number flashing on my phone screen every couple of days. He doesn't leave voice or text messages. I don't call back, but send a message asking him not to contact me. A clean slice through the past we share makes sense. Is this wrong of me? Possibly, but the only way I can cope is to gather everything that I let spill out and push the emotions back inside myself. Guy returns an 'I understand' message and tells me he's in hospital.

A week later, Lottie calls me. I don't recognise the number and, thinking the call is work related, I answer.

"Hello, Phe?"

"Who's this?"

"Lottie. I'm calling on behalf of Noah."

Noah. I blink away the last images I have of him, confused and lost. "What do you mean on behalf of him?"

"He's worried about you. I told him to leave this, that your relationship's over and he understands. But I think it would help if I could tell him you're okay."

"Tell Guy I'm fine and to worry about himself."

I consider ending the call. I don't want to snap back to thoughts of Guy again.

"Noah stopped taking his medication a couple of months ago, that's what happened," Lottie explains.

"No, what happened is he told me his name is Guy and that he's dying," I snap back. "I have no idea about his motivation behind doing this but I hope that helps you understand why I don't want to see or hear from him again." I pause, aware how cold I sound. "Sorry, I hope he's going okay but I've been unwell too. I'm too fragile to deal with what has happened between us."

"I do understand," she says softly. "Noah's better than he was now he's back in hospital. Once his medication is stable again, he'll be good. I hope you can see this was what caused his behaviour."

"Not all of his behaviour. Guy was unwell but he wasn't totally irrational, he was functioning enough to keep the truth hidden. He had many chances to explain, but he carried on lying to me. I could've helped him. Has he told you our full story?"

"No. He won't tell me much about you but he says he's talking to his psychologist about why he behaved as he did."

"I'm sorry, Lottie. I don't have the strength to risk becoming close to Guy again. I need to forget about him."

"I think he understands that."

I close my eyes and inhale. "He's alright though?"

"He'll be fine. This is the worst he's been for years. I think his father's death last year compounded the situation he was in a couple of years before and he never grieved properly. I'm confident he'll get back to normal again."

Normal? What is normal? To him or to anybody? Lottie speaks with such conviction and holds the key to unlocking the box holding more of Guy's secrets. I waver. I could ask to speak to him, but then what?

No. I may have lost my travelling companion, but my road ahead is clearer.

CHAPTER THIRTY

My sessions with the psychologist delve deeper than before. My past conversations with Guy dug into the buried fears and thoughts, and pushed them to the surface. For the first time in therapy, I let go of the guilt about my family's deaths, frame my life with what I want and need, instead of what is expected. I never appreciated how my confidence at work increased recently, or how my ability to stand up for myself and not accept unfounded criticism improved. Talking to the psychologist painted a picture of the person I'm becoming.

My response to Guy's betrayal, my refusal to let this pull me into a black hole, demonstrates the strength Guy gave me, and that confuses me a hell of a lot.

I join Jen on nights out, become part of her social circle but this is the one place I hover on the edge. Guy has nipped in the bud any desire to start a relationship. I want to spend time dictating my own life. Finally, I'm in control but in a different way; the need to micromanage my life slips into an ability to trust myself.

My latest session with a psychologist at the clinic passes in conversation rather than analysis, and she suggests we cut the sessions to monthly – then less. Several months of therapy and I'm finally coming to the end. I hope one day I might even be free of the medication. Whatever happens, I can't imagine being back where I was seven months ago.

Outside, much needed rain deluges the carpark. When I arrived earlier the clouds in the sky were sparse, and as I look up the irony hits. In the quiet room with Cathy, my dark clouds lifted but out here, I step back into them. Life moves on as fast as the clouds travel above me and I will live that life to the fullest.

Rain bounces off the tarmac and as I have no jacket or umbrella, I head to find the small hospital cafe to wait for the storm to pass. The bright lobby holds two elevators and several large signs listing the doctors and departments in the large private hospital. A couple pass, the woman heavily pregnant, her shoes squelching while her partner fusses over her. I smile at them and step out of the way, as I continue to look for the direction I need to go.

I'm about to head to the low wooden reception desk when a nearby figure catches my attention. A tall man with blond hair heads down the carpeted hallway in my direction.

Guy stops when he sees me. A man weaves past, Guy's sudden stop almost tripping him.

My mouth dries at the sight of him. This is the first time I've seen him in almost six weeks. He approaches with a wary smile, the dimples digging into his cheeks. Guy's face has lost the pallor of last time I saw him, his hair growing back to the length of the night we met.

"Hello, Phe," he says quietly. "How are you?"

"I'm fine. Looking for the cafe." The words come from my mouth, but I'm unaware of anything but my heart whooshing blood into my ears. The Guy I've held in my mind is the sick man who told me his horrific secret, in turn indicating how little I meant to him. The one in front of me now is the old Guy. The one I loved.

He wrinkles his nose. "Don't. The coffee is bad. You're better off finding a place nearby."

We regard each other warily as the rain bounces off the forecourt to the hospital and I incline my head. "I'm killing time until that stops."

"Good idea."

A woman holding a small child's hand and pushing a stroller appears, wrangling the child into the elevator. I step out of the way, aware we're obstructing the doors but Guy stays and holds the heavy metal door open, ensuring they don't close on the little boy heading in after her.

"Thank you," she says and gives Guy a smile.

"No worries," he replies.

Guy steps away again and my heart leaps a little at the man who's naturally a gentleman, not missing the subtle second glance the mother gives him.

"You're not ill again are you?" he asks, frowning.

"Psychologist."

"Oh. Helping?"

"Yes. Immensely." I pause. "You?"

"Psychiatrist."

"All the psychs," I say with a weak smile.

Guy digs his hand into his black jacket pockets. "We always meet in the strangest of places."

"Right." I rub my cheek, unsure what happens next. A voice inside urges me to run, but a different voice whispers to stay and talk. "Thank you."

"What for?"

"Showing me the way to travel."

A muscle twitches in Guy's cheek. "It was a fun journey with you. I'm glad you carried on and didn't fall off the path."

I laugh. "You love your metaphors, don't you?"

"Life is one big metaphor." He grins. "How's the bucket list?"

I stiffen. "Fine. How's yours?"

"I tore the list up, Phe," he says softly. "So, thank you."

"What did I do?"

"You showed me a new direction."

How can an ordinary moment hold so much? We're in public, in reality, but all I feel is the rope tightening around us again. I battle against reaching out to Guy; annoyed I want his touch too. Look at us. We would never have worked.

"You mean you've changed your mind about your lack of future?" I ask.

"I've decided to follow your example and not run from what the future holds." He sighs. "I'm accepting that I *have* this... illness and not that I *am* this."

"And working through the issues with your past?"

"Are you?"

I laugh. "What a weird conversation and strange place to have it."

Guy takes my elbow, the way he did at the masquerade ball and guides me to a seating area. Two upholstered armchairs and a low round table are situated near the window at the front of the hospital. His touch triggers the past, sweeping away the last few weeks. When he sits, I join him. Guy leans forward, elbows on his knees, cupping his chin in both hands.

"I am very sorry about what I did," he says. "About the lies."

I'm caught in the swell again, Guy's presence the real reason I've stayed away. He is more than his illness, as I'm more than mine. But this strange sensation that seeing him again has reconnected me with a missing piece of my soul is washed away by the doubt I could ever trust him again.

"I would say it's fine, but it's not, Guy. But thank you for apologising."

"I tried to talk to you and explain, but you wouldn't answer my calls."

I sit on my hands. "I couldn't. I didn't know you. You weren't the man I loved."

The rain pelts the outside world; cool air blasts my back as the nearby glass entrance doors slide open. I keep my eyes fixed on the window, convincing myself the blurring is the rain and not my eyes.

"I understand." His voice is loaded with sincerity and sorrow. "I missed you," he says, the words barely audible. "I regret not telling you the truth every minute of every day since you walked away."

"Why didn't you tell me at the beginning?"

"I thought you'd run. You had your own mental health issues. I didn't think you'd want a relationship with a man who has his own."

"Wrong, I didn't want a relationship with a man who lied to me. When I think about what you hid and what you planned to do, I feel sick." I look into his deep-water eyes. "What hurts the most is you couldn't ask me for help."

"I did the wrong thing. I stopped taking my meds because I felt better around you. I thought I could be well and then I'd deserve you."

"I would've accepted you. Everything about you, apart from the plan to end your life."

"I think I'd already changed my mind about that," he says with a small smile. "A few weeks with you and the plans began to unravel. Until the voices came back to remind me."

"And now?"

"The voices ruined everything and then they left. I should never have stopped the meds." The low round table between us is a barrier against the possibility of physical contact. Am I relieved or unhappy about that? What would I do if he reached out? "But I don't know if I'll be Noah again, even if he isn't the bad guy anymore."

"I prefer when you're just some guy. I like him."

Guy laughs, eyes lighting up. "Guy was happier, until I fucked up." His phone beeps and he pulls it from his jacket. He glances at the text. "Crap. Sorry. I have to go."

"Oh. Right."

He stands. "You need a ride somewhere? I can drop you on the way."

The downpour continues, a vertical sheet of water from the sky with no sign of a break. Ten minutes to the bus, ten minutes from the bus to my house. In the rain.

But can I go with Guy and resist asking to see him again? I stand too, almost knocking into Guy and he steadies my arm. The ocean scent reaches over to me, pulling up memories of his skin against mine.

Guy zips up his black canvas jacket. "Okay?"

"Yes. Thanks."

We step into the arched entrance, the wind blowing the water toward us and I shiver in my thin jacket. Guy's presence sends a mix of emotions, releasing ones I don't want.

I can't go with him.

"I think I'll take the bus," I say.

He steps to one side. "Right. You sure?"

"Probably best."

"Probably."

I shiver as the wind pushes against my thin coat. "Are you still going to England next month?"

"Are you?"

"I don't think so." I've considered this over and over, changed my mind numerous times. Some days the idea of continuing my journey appeals, others I'm constrained by the Phe lurking beneath – the one filled with anxiety and doubt. Could I travel so far alone?

Guy nods and chews on his lip. "Going was on my bucket list. The one that doesn't exist anymore, remember? So I can't."

"Sorry, I didn't think."

We exchange more awkward smiles, and Guy digs his hands into his jacket pockets again. "Well, I guess I'll see you around, Phe."

"Yes, we can hang out in the psych ward together."

"I don't think things will come to that again, will they?"

I don't know. Will they? "Bye, Guy. Noah."

Why am I fighting tears? When I walked away last time, I didn't feel the wrench I do now. The pain in Guy's eyes from that day is replaced by hope; hope dimming as I look away again.

"Guy. For you, I'm Guy."

Terrified the emotions will deluge me along with the rain, I step out onto the tarmac to cross the road, eyes blurring. A car screeches to a halt in front of me. At the same time, Guy yanks me by the arm and onto the pavement.

"I thought you said you'd lost your death wish?" he asks.

"Funny."

The rain flattens my hair, dripping down my nose and Guy blinks raindrops from his long lashes. "How's your bucket list going?"

"I went surfing. I'm having lessons."

"Wow. That's awesome, Phe. Well done."

I shrug my shoulders. "You got me halfway there."

"I did." Guy extends a hand and wipes rain from my cheek, his cold fingers resting on my skin as he looks at me. "I'm always happy to help with your list even though I've ditched mine."

"I'm amazed at how much I've done in just a few months."

He grins. "Write another. Bigger challenges. Overseas."

I pace from one foot to the other as the water splashes across my feet; we can't talk about lists. "I should go."

"Of course."

I don't want to walk away; no longer aware of anything but the possibility of reaching out to the man whose presence reminds me he stopped me sinking under.

"Number five," he whispers.

I don't have a chance to reply before Guy's mouth meets my lips, a raindrop from his nose touching mine at the same time. His lips are cool and familiar, the softness becoming firm as I press mine on his in return.

I pull away before the kiss deepens. We stand, fingers on each other's cheeks, and my heart aches because I can't do what we both want. He's connected to a part of myself I'm cutting away: naïve, scared, and confused. But then he's also responsible for pulling the new Phe away from her. His face shines in the rain, the radiance in his smile not matched by the sad understanding in his eyes.

"Life's never like the movies, is it?" he asks and shakes water from his jacket.

"No."

A car splashes through the water nearby and a woman climbs out, onto the pavement next to us. The curious look she gives pushes back in my awareness that I'm in the rain outside a hospital with a man I never wanted to see again. A man whose kiss reunited me with a part of myself that he'll never give back.

"Keep your head above the water, Ophelia," he whispers and brushes his lips against my mouth, scruff scraping my cheek.

Something has filled my throat with cotton wool, absorbing the words. I have this moment to ask Guy to stay, to go somewhere and talk, but I can't speak.

He sighs. "I understand what you're saying by not saying anything. My number hasn't changed if you want to meet up sometime. But I totally understand why this should be a hello and goodbye."

"Okay," I manage to whisper.

Guy touches my cheek one last time, brushing water from my skin. "Do you know what's special about kissing in the rain?" Mutely, I shake my head. "Loving somebody is easy when the sun is shining, but when you're caught in the storm, you discover who's prepared to stand with you. I'll be there again if you need me."

I'm seconds away from asking him to wait, when Guy turns away and sprints across the road to the car park. I fight against calling after him but he's right. Life is never like the movies.

CHAPTER THIRTY-ONE

One Month Later

#7 Learn to surf

I'm above the ocean, closer than the last time, and ready to fight the waves. But the water no longer controls me. I'm not frightened anymore. I paddle the surfboard through the water, striving to catch the waves that have eluded me for the last ten minutes. The exhilaration and joy of surfing is my new natural high.

I spot one, advancing closer and hope rises, a determination to hit the wave and clear out the negative energy that's built up this week. I'm considering moving closer to the beach, and coming here more often. The anxiety is now excitement, the fear: exhilaration.

I pull myself onto the board, the wax beneath my feet pushing between my toes as I turn the board into the wave, and suddenly, I'm on top of the water. Nature's energy is beneath my feet, taking me, but not pulling me down. I'm flying above the world, the way I imagined as a child; like a bird riding on the wind. Time washes away, as I escape from reality until the world is just me and the wave.

Water sprays into my face, as I become one with

what I once fought. Finally, I accept the danger of life and chase it. Weightlessness takes over as I speed up and head towards shore. The power of the wave pushes my board and I move across, up and down the face, gaining speed. All my senses belong to nature – the air rushing by, the sound of the wave breaking as water sprays around, and a seagull crying overhead.

These days, when I swim the deep water it's to ride above and not to be pulled beneath.

On the shore, I stand with my board and no other thought than to paddle out again. I know I'll keep going until my body won't let me, then go home with muscles aching and exhausted. All I'll want to do tomorrow is come back.

I wave to my fellow surfers. I've been surfing for a couple of months now and some days I stay and chat, discussing waves and the best places to go, but not today. I'm planning to go further afield, for a weekend with a group soon. Ironic how the girl terrified of water now spends so much of her free time submerged in the world of surfing.

Today, I see Guy, his tall figure as recognisable as the custom board he once tried to persuade me to use. I know Guy sees me too because he pauses. Since the day we met at the hospital, I've thought about him often. The Guy I met that day was different to the one I'd known all along, perhaps because he was the real Guy, not hiding behind exuberance as he tried vainly to keep afloat. I understand that people can become well and change; but I have so many questions unanswered – am I too fragile to risk seeing Guy again or stronger than I think?

I haven't spoken to Guy since the meeting last month, and now fate throws us together for a second time. There was always the chance we'd meet and although I spend time craving to share this experience with the man who taught me to let go, I can't bring myself to forgive him for the betrayal.

My mind travels in circles in attempts to decipher why he lied and for so long, at how unwell he was, and should I have accepted he can get better? But when somebody tells you they intend to kill themselves in the same breath as telling you he loves you, how could I? My suicidal thoughts were a blip; his was a long-standing plan. How is that easy to let go; for me or for him?

I wait until Guy is in the water, seeking his own seconds of freedom, and leave.

CHAPTER THIRTY-TWO

The winter sun shines through the window, across my desk, and I cradle my cup of mocha as I sort through my morning work emails. Next to me, open to page 14, is a copy of this month's magazine. Page 14 and 15 are covered by an article. My article. Not about face creams or the latest diets, but about my breakdown and recovery. No, the whole story isn't there; twenty-one years of my life can't be condensed into clever copy. My experience is a basis for interviewing other women my age about the pressures of adulthood, a kickback against the selfish Gen Y label.

If this resonates with one person who then looks for help, rather than find themselves hanging on the edge in a place where there isn't a Guy with flowers waiting, I've succeeded.

I re-read the article for the tenth time. Similar copy is on the website inviting comments, but the printed copy is physical. In my hand. I reach the end and the final line that chokes me each time. "Don't wait your whole life for a Prince Charming to bring you a happy ever after, find your own."

Does Guy follow the magazine's website? Has he seen himself in my words? Guy once said he checked out the website, but I could be a painful memory for him too.

Erica shared my excitement and people have approached me asking if the story is true – if the man with the flowers exists. I smile and give a vague answer, adding in something about artistic licence.

Guy. I glance at the date on my desktop. July 8th. Our planned trip to England was due to start this weekend. Last weekend, I opened a drawer and found Guy's odd sketch, a map of the UK with landmarks artfully doodled, a dotted red line from place to place. I remembered discussions and arguments about where we would go – his desire for history and the country versus mine for the modern, and the compromises we were setting.

This triggered the ache, the one I submerge the majority of the time. Seeing him at the beach over the weekend, even though we didn't speak, prompted memories of our conversations

The knifelike pain to my chest that hit the day Guy sliced me open with his lies lessens, but never stops. If I take away his deception, Guy is the one person in my life who I clicked with.

When Guy reached out to the raw Ophelia, he took hold of more than just her heart. Not having to pretend around Guy meant I became the girl who drowned with her family, and lost the shell of a person who survived.

Although I can never be Lia again, and never want to be Ophelia, he made it okay to be Phe.

CHAPTER THIRTY-THREE

The doors glide closed behind, shutting out the last breath of the Perth winter air. I stand at the edge of the airport terminal and drop my heavy rucksack on the floor. Rubbing my shoulder, I take a deep breath then exhale the doubt. I can do this. I moved across Australia to start a career on my own; a trip to England is nothing. Temporary. Exciting. New experiences that I denied myself open to me, a bucket list item ticked.

A family pushes past, suitcases trundling loudly over the tiled floor as they wrangle two small children. The blonde-haired girl's wide-eyed awe contrasts with her older brother's pursed lips. I edge to one side, to avoid being bumped again. The steady stream of arrivals passes by as I remain still and scan the hall for the check-in desk.

Locating the correct queue, I shuffle my heavy rucksack along the floor. I'm a late arrival, which is unlike me, but I watched the clock at home, as I debated whether to go ahead with this. I've long since taken my bucket list from the fridge, but now have the folded paper tucked into a pocket inside the rucksack.

Unable to forget him and how close we came to reuniting, I almost called Guy to ask if he'd come too. Then I remembered the last time we saw each other, Guy told me he'd given up on his bucket list, which includes our planned trip abroad. Calling Guy and asking him to come would be unfair, pulling him backwards when he's clearly moved on.

The girl at the check-in desk takes my ticket and passport as if I have no right to be here, making a loud comment about how check-in was due to close in a minutes time. I smile even though my heart pounds with the fear I might miss the flight.

I hurry through Security, up the escalator, carrying a small bag with my essentials – phone, book, passport, money. The old Phe with her anxiety over whether I've remembered everything resurfaces; but she has her checklist tucked into her bag next to the bucket list.

Stragglers pass through my plane's boarding gate, and I sink my shoulders with the relief there isn't a plane full of people waiting for me. I glance at the screen with boarding times and frown. I'm not as late as the stupid girl on check-in made out.

The dark-haired man on the gate has a genuine warmth; perhaps he enjoys his job more than the girl downstairs. He takes my boarding pass in manicured fingers; and when he smiles, his dimples kick in another reminder of Guy.

"I'm not the last then?" I ask, short of breath from my panicked travels through the terminal.

"Not at all, there're a few behind you. I hope they leave the bar soon." He winks at me and I smile back.

Only once I sit in the narrow seat by the window, bag stowed above me, do I relax. I gaze at the tarmac below and the ant-like airline staff loading the luggage onto the plane; and for the first time, excitement fills my body instead of nerves. Somebody once told me anxiety and fear are the same chemical reaction, and how I interpreted the sensation pinpointed which it was. I'm unsure I agree; excitement can't come without nerves.

I spot a picture of London on the front of the airline magazine and pull it from the seat pocket, flicking through to the article.

A fellow passenger sits next to me and focused on the text, critically analysing the article as I always do, I twist to one side to avoid contact.

"If I go to London with you, will you promise to come to Scotland?"

I jerk my head up at the voice. Guy. He points at the magazine in my trembling hands. "You know I don't like heights, right? I'm not sure I can go on that big Ferris wheel thing."

"London Eye," I squeak.

"Yeah, that." He shuffles in his seat and rests his head on the back. "Wasn't sure you'd come."

I stare at the apparition. He looks straight ahead, with a relaxed smile on his face. Blond hair touches his ears and when he moved, the familiar scent of his safety and warmth reached me. I grasp at words. "You said you weren't doing anything else on your list; I didn't think you were still going."

"I don't have a list. I'm travelling." He turns in his seat, leg brushing mine. "Travelling companions?"

My skin goosebumps under his scrutiny, the dark blue eyes dragging me back to who we were. He reaches out a hand and folds it around mine, reconnecting.

"We knew we'd both be here, didn't we?" he asks softly. "I did. I knew if you were here that we were meant to travel together again."

"Yes." I bite inside my cheek, stopping the stream of words fighting to come out of my mouth. Yes, I'd hoped Guy would be here and denied that hope is what drove me to this time and place.

Guy runs his thumb across the back of my hand and I squeeze his fingers. Why did I leave this so long? I could've contacted him after the kiss at the hospital but never did.

We remain in silence, holding hands as the cabin crew walk up and down checking the passengers' seat belts are fastened. Head already spinning from the fact I made it to the airport, Guy's presence has taken me from spaced out to sky high. My palms sweat beneath his.

"Are you scared of flying?" he asks as the engines rumble to life beneath us.

"No. Are you?"

"Last plane I was on I jumped out of, hopefully I'll stay inside this one."

I turn to him, cheeks heating as my chest constricts with the happiness of seeing him. Guy reaches out with his other hand and smooths my hair.

"You think sometimes life could be like the movies?" he asks. "Can I kiss the girl and kill the bad guys?"

"Who are the bad guys?"

He shrugs. "Who knows? I'll just do the 'kiss the girl' part."

Guy places his lips on mine and, in an awkward embrace, obstructed by airline seats and seatbelts, we kiss. His mouth is familiar, his taste and touch pulling me back down to earth as the plane gathers speed along the runway. Who knows if the take-off is what lurches my stomach, or the sheer emotion of being back with the man who set me on the path I'm on.

The plane lurches, tipping to one side and I bury my face in Guy's chest, inhaling his warmth, and ignore my confusion. Guy rests his chin on my head, rubbing my back. "I'm not running away from the future anymore, Phe. I want to make one. With you."

"Why didn't you call me?"

"I was scared you'd say no."

I look up at him. "What if I'd said no when you sat down next to me today?"

"Then I'd spend the next twenty hours explaining why you should say yes."

I groan and he flashes the dimpled smile I've missed. "I knew if you were here, you'd already said yes."

"And I knew if you were here, I could never say no."

The seatbelt light flicks off and I shift so I'm closer to Guy. "I think we should start a new journey," he whispers. "And this time I know where I'm going."

CHAPTER THIRTY-FOUR

#3 Visit London
#6 See the Van Gogh painting, Sunflowers.

I sit on the low wooden bench as Guy stands a few feet away in front of the painting. Other tourists spread around the room, talking in low voices as they move slowly from painting to painting. Guy remains in one place for several minutes, behind the red cordon, as if held in place. I smile to myself as a couple of teenage girls switch their attention from the masterpieces to the tall, muscular man, with his hands in jeans pockets, oblivious to their interest. I have a great view of his rear, while they can appreciate his face is as big an attraction as his body. I blink back to viewing Guy as the man who held me, whose mouth touched every inch of my skin and whose eyes held as much love as pain. The man I loved.

Everybody knows the sunflower paintings, judging by the number of people they're a big draw card for the gallery. I'm not a fan of art, so today's visit to the National Gallery in London didn't appeal. However, my desire to reconnect with Guy for a couple of days before heading off on my planned trip to other parts of the UK pushed me to come here too. Things are easy-going between us again, the hours seated together in an airplane reforging the old 'us', but can I take this a step further and allow myself close? Our long flight involved even longer conversations, but many topics were skirted around.

I told Guy he still has secrets to give up, that he needs to now answer every question that I should've asked before. He's well now; this Guy is the man who strolled toward me at the café the second time we met – as vibrant as the art we've studied today. The other man who told me he wanted to die in the same breath as he told me he loved me isn't here. But what if this man with me now is him – Noah – and only Guy loved me?

Last night, after we arrived at the London hotel, Guy told me the story about his sister, Sally. The words were hard for him and the emotion raw in his voice as he recounted the day he found her in bed, crying because she had a bad headache. He was eight. Sally was four. Nobody else was around and he wanted to look after her. Guy managed to open the bottle of medicine his nanny usually gave him when he was sick and gave Sally a few spoonfuls. Then he tucked Sally into bed, to get better, not wanting to disturb anybody else. She never did; Sally died.

For much of Guy's life he believed he'd killed his sister, that the decision to medicate her had poisoned Sally. Guy's dad blamed his young son too, mixed up in his mind with his wife's death, but years later Guy discovered she'd died of meningitis. The sick Guy refused to believe this, instead convincing himself they'd lied to stop his guilt. In his mind, the decision not to find an adult to help, but instead try to nurse her caused his sister's death.

I listened in horror and reached out to him. Guy refused to look at me through most of the story, clearly, he still struggles to come to terms with this part of his past. But he now believes he wasn't responsible, and that's what matters.

I look over. The man blending in like any other tourist needs to give up the rest of his secrets so I can move on – with or without him.

Guy approaches. "Aren't you having a closer look at the paintings?"

"I will. The room's claustrophobic with people crowded around."

"How about I buy you a tea towel with the sunflowers on, then you can look at the picture whenever you want?" He holds out a hand.

"I think I'd prefer a mug." I grasp his fingers and he pulls me to my feet. "So, how does it feel to see the painting that inspired you to paint?"

"Amazing. This place is incredible. I could stay here all day." His smile widens at my poor attempt to disguise boredom. "Don't panic, I won't make you. Come on, I'll buy you a tea towel."

"Mug. And don't forget, you're going on the London Eye with me later."

"You'll have to hold my hand."

I lace my fingers through his. "Of course."

Guy stops at the entrance to the gift shop, and I shake my head. "I was joking about the mug, I'm not carrying that around England for several weeks."

"Okay, I want to buy a souvenir though. I doubt I'll be visiting here again in a hurry."

I peer through the doorway at the racks of cards and huge prints of artwork on the walls. People edge around each other in the busy shop, selecting their spoils.

"I'll meet you at the cafe, I think."

Guy laughs at me. "No worries." He kisses my forehead.

I watch him for a moment as he heads into the store, confused by how naturally our lives have fitted back together. His easy-going nature was often at the fore, and with his dark side gone I can almost believe he's my Guy again. Almost.

I find my way downstairs away from the quiet calm of the gallery and into one of the nearby cafes, where I order two coffees from the counter beneath the bright orange walls. The cafe is as busy as the rest of the gallery but I scout out a corner decorated with large black leather seats beneath small paintings. I sip my mocha as I wait for Guy.

He reappears, holding a plastic bag printed with the Gallery logo. When Guy sits, he rummages inside and pulls out a tea towel. "There you go."

I groan and fold it onto my knee, looking back at Guy's dimpled grin. "Thank you. I bought you a coffee."

Guy sits and shuffles across the leather seat. As he sips his drink, he lapses into silence. I know why. I squeeze his hand in an unspoken gesture that everything is okay.

"I guess there're a few things I need to explain to you," he says softly.

Do I want to know this? Be pulled back? Half of me doesn't want him to, but that's the half who didn't ask the questions once before. "Here?"

"I can't hold onto this any longer."

"Is what you need to tell me so bad you need us to be in public, and I can't freak out?" I say and poke him in the side.

He doesn't laugh. "About things I've said in the past, we both skirted around discussing everything on the plane. Didn't we?"

"Like we usually do."

"And we have to talk or this won't work. We won't fix this until there're no secrets left."

"Okay."

He places his cup on the low table. "I lied by omission, but I also lied, period. Some things are true: my father did die and leave me money, my mother did die in childbirth, and I am both Noah and Guy. Some of what I said wasn't true. When I got sick again I believed what I told you, such as the crazy idea my dad invented the internet." His voice is hushed, below the quiet voices of others in the room.

"I didn't think that was true about your dad."

He takes my hand. "My father left me with my grandparents after my sister died. He moved away to the States for a couple of years. He came back, but he never allowed me close to him. I was looked after by a string of nannies. I invented a reason for his lack of love and disappearance, to explain why he had to leave and was busy all the time. My father did work in the 'dotcom' field early on and made a crap load of money. Money I now have."

A couple of fellow tourists sit at a table next to us, chattering in Japanese as they stir sugar into coffee.

"And I am well again now. Stable. I've decided to plan a future outside of myself. Find a job." Guy glances at the couple and lowers his voice. "The last thing. I've struggled against telling you this for months. You'll either walk away, or understand, which is why I'm telling you now, before we get closer. I don't want to lose you."

"What?" I ask and squeeze his fingers.

"How we met. I believe that was fate, as I've told you before, but I never told you why I was really there."

My stomach lurches, hair standing up on my arms the way the breeze caused the night on the rocks. "Were you planning to jump too?" I whisper.

"No." Guy drags a hand down his face and doesn't speak, mouth forming words he won't say. "I was bringing flowers to the spot you chose. I never expected anybody else to be there."

The one obvious reason for this springs into my mind and I look back at him, eyes widening. "Who died there, Guy? Your dad?"

"No. He died of a heart attack last year, although I think his heart never mended after Mum died."

The familiar fear that Guy will tell me something I don't want to hear returns. Can I keep doing this? "Who died?" For a moment Guy stares ahead in an all too familiar way. The battle against speaking the words is evident on his strained face. I place a hand over his. "Tell me."

"My girlfriend. Ex. She wasn't really my girlfriend. I never loved her not like I love –" He stops himself. "Emma loved me, but I was sick, pushed her away. I didn't have the capacity to feel what she wanted me to."

"And she... There?" I close my eyes, focusing on pushing down the rising emotion, controlling the effect of his words.

"Yes. Three years ago to that day we met."

My eyes remain closed, fighting the image of a girl falling to her death. I pull my hand from his, perspiration breaking out across my skin. "You didn't save her, so you wanted to save me instead," I say in a low voice. "You pushed away your guilt by making me into her, is that what happened?"

"No. Never. You were never her in my mind. Not once." His expression is hard, as emphatic as his voice.

"Why then?"

"Do you think I'd walk away and leave somebody who was about to kill themselves?" he asks hoarsely. "I'd already caused three deaths. Didn't matter who you were – man or woman, old or young – I wasn't leaving without you."

"But then afterwards. You drew me into your life, taught me to move on and live. You did all that because you wanted to fix what you thought you'd caused!" I bite back my rising tone, and raise my head to look at Guy.

"No, Phe. That's not right. We clicked. The closer we became and the happier we both were, the further I was from being Noah. Noah caused all the problems. That's why I was Guy. Am Guy."

I take a ragged breath. Was I somebody else to Guy all along? He says I wasn't, but how can I believe that? I set down my cup and stare at my hands in my lap. Jet lag adds to the surreality of the words, there's an increased distance between me and the real world.

"Phe, listen to me." Cautiously he reaches out and

I cross my arms against my chest, blinking away tears. "I'm sorry what I'm saying is upsetting you, but I had to tell you. You don't understand how important you are or how you've changed me. Why does how we met matter? The only thing I take from that is we were *meant* to meet."

"Every time I think I understand, you confuse me further, Guy."

"I didn't have to tell you the truth, but I did. I never want to keep secrets again. They eat away at my reality." Guy shifts closer. "I want you to be my reality."

"I fell in love with you, and I didn't want to. You hurt me." I hold my hand to my chest. "You don't understand how much. I'm taking a big risk here by letting you back in."

"I know and I'm sorry, but I boarded the plane yesterday to fight for what I believed in. You. Me. Us."

I blink back at him, heart aching. Not from his words but because I'm scared of falling under again. "Could this work? We're both a mess."

"*Were* a mess. Can we start again? Something brought us together and never allowed us to completely let go."

"I want to but I'm so confused. I missed you, I wanted you to be there yesterday. This feels right but –"

"We started our journey again." Guy takes my arms and pulls so I have to uncross them. "Look at me." The man with the eyes that threatened to drown me looks back, the intensity drawing me close. "I love you."

I choke on my words, tears welling. "I'm frightened of loving you again."

Guy drops his hands from my arms.

"I know I hurt you, you let me in, told me your story and I never told you mine. I came back because I hoped you'd want me to fight for you. For us. I've told you my secrets, even the ones I hid from the world. You have all of me now. I don't think I could ever give myself to somebody else." He cups my cheek. "Phe, once, I thought I was a whole person and I hated that person. Then I met you and realised I had a second part and she completed me. The problem is, I lost you. That's why I'm fighting for you now."

I close my eyes and breathe deeply, fitting the jigsaw pieces together in my head. His girlfriend. His mum. His sister. I know everything now and if I judge him for this I'm as bad as the words he once told himself. There's a huge reason why I need to draw a line under that night, forever.

"I don't understand why I felt complete with you, even when I knew you hid parts of yourself. Now I'm scared that this Guy is too different to the one I fell in love with, that we can't be two halves the way we were."

"We're two parts who make a whole, otherwise why would we be here again, now."

His words are spoken as a fact and not a question, followed immediately by his lips on mine. Guy tips my face toward his, long fingers under my chin. Everything is stripped away now, back to a rawness of souls who share an understanding in each other's touch. Guy places his mouth on mine; lips soft at first until I kiss him back, holding his head. Guy's kiss reaches into the place inside me where my love for him still lives, and fills the emptiness with his.

"I'm glad you were there," I whisper and touch his cheek.

"On the plane?"

"No, on the night you saved my life. Maybe part of me already knew there was a world I belonged to, one you lived in too."

"And we can go back there?" he asks.

"There's a lot more life to explore together."

"Travelling companions," he says with a grin.

"In our world and theirs."

I wrap myself in his arms, the outside world retreating. Who cares what came before? We live for what happens next. Guy is my second part, his world clicking into place with mine as my body melds with his through our embrace. The fusion of our lives happened months ago, in the moment I walked away from death and into a new future.

This man brought me life and light, risked himself as he fought against the darkness. Even when lost, he fiercely held onto his belief in us.

EPILOGUE

"Every man dies, but not every man really lives."
- Sir William Wallace

The waves fought me today, elusive and frustrating, but I refused to let the ocean win. Guy wanted to head to Margaret River where surfers had circulated news of the monster waves left by the retreating storm. He showed me the images on his phone, waves as tall as a multi-storey building towering over a surfer you could barely see. I told him I may have conquered my fear of water, but I'd also conquered my death wish too. Guy wrinkled his nose and wandered around the house for a few minutes, debating what to do and eventually we headed to our favourite local spot for catching waves.

In the moment when the wave is beneath my board, I'm lost in a world created by the battle for those few seconds before the ride ends. I'm here with Guy but we are chasing a high we can only achieve separately. Rivalry breaks out as he catches more waves than I do, his years of experience outdoing my year on a learning curve as steep as the ocean I ride.

The trip to the UK continued, and with our secrets out, we stepped onward and left them behind.

Since we returned to Australia, our growing closeness over the months has cemented into a loving, trusting relationship. Our relationship likely has less secrets than the everyday people who've never struggled in the depths. Our hearts and souls are anchored together to fight the inevitable storms we'll face in the future.

I drag my board to the shore and drop it on the sand, aching after finally replacing the frustration with elation. I scan the beach for Guy and we see each other at the same time. This is a casual day; he's in boardies and rash vest rather than his wetsuit he wears when serious surfing has to be done. I still expect him to disappear south to catch the monster waves and I'll let him go, of course.

Guy watches as I approach, reaching out to hold my damp head and kiss me with his warm lips. His growing fringe tickles my forehead as I tiptoe to press my lips harder against his. In response, he circles an arm around me.

"Finally caught one?" he asks, eyes glinting.

"I always do."

"You never give up, that's one of the things I love about you." He brushes his mouth against mine again.

"One of many I hope."

His hand roams around to my ass and drags me against his hips. "One of very many."

Slapping Guy's hand away, I drag a towel from the top of the nearby rucksack. I spread the towel onto the sand, and sit to take weight off my tired legs. Guy sits next to me and passes a bottle of water. The Indian Ocean churns, hiding the cerulean blue beneath the white crests of the waves. The Perth summer sun heats my bare arms, drying my pink rash vest.

"I never thought I'd find peace in the water," I say half to myself and rest my head on Guy's shoulder. "I love my life with you. I'm a world away from the girl I was a year ago. Thank you."

"You know that you saved my life too, Phe," he whispers and rests his damp hair against mine. "I think that makes us quits."

I nudge his arm so he has to wrap his strength around me. "Just promise me you'll never try to be my Prince Charming," I whisper.

"I'm happy to be just some Guy, if he's your guy."

Guy never returned to his old name, arguing Noah is the sick part of himself when he's uncontrolled and that Guy was the man who found peace with me. His remaining family are wary, worried he'll struggle again and that between us we'll create a perfect storm of mental illness which will drown us both. What they don't understand is the depth of our understanding of each other; the intuition into Guy I now have would head off this situation. We've made a commitment to never be alone at a point of no return; a promise we'll tell each other if we're heading there.

The only place we're moving to now is into a new life.

"I love you," I whisper and look around, ensuring he really sees and doesn't just hear.

Guy strokes tendrils of damp hair from my face and rests his fingertips on my cheek. "And I love you. Always."

"If we were a movie, which one do you think we'd be?" I ask, trickling sand through my fingers.

"Our life isn't like the movies, remember? In those, the story ends with a happy ever after."

"Are you saying we won't have a happy ever after?" I ask and smack his leg.

"No, because this story is nowhere near the end. This is just the beginning. Stories have to end to have a happy ever after."

Our original story began with pain and confusion, surrounded by darkness and fear of the future. But stories, like the future, can be rewritten. Fate has a hand in pulling people together, and sometimes the reasons why make no sense until months later. Fate brought Guy to me on the night he saved my life, unaware that I would save his.

We have love. We have understanding. We have acceptance. Not only for each other, but more importantly, for ourselves.

We have a future that stretches far beyond twenty items on a list.

Swimming the same deep water as Guy is hard, but struggling in the depths with him is better than losing myself amongst those who never find their way out of the shallows.

The Same Deep Water

Lisa Swallow

Acknowledgements

As always, a big thank you to my beta readers: Louise and Leeann. Also thanks to Demelza, Sasha, Cassi and Shelley for last-minute input.

This stunning cover was designed by the amazing Najla Qamber. Thank you again for making my book look outstanding!

Thank you to Peggy and Becky from Hot Tree Editing.

Thanks to Nicole from Indiesage for taking over the promotion and release and to Inkslinger for organising a tour.

Thank you Rebecca Hamilton for your advice and for sharing your knowledge.

A huge thank you to all the bloggers who continue to support me, I couldn't reach as many people as I do without your help. Every single post, share and shout out means a lot.

To my friends in the Lounge: you ladies keep me sane and make me laugh and I feel I've made so many new friends. When times were tough this year you've helped me through in more ways than you imagine. Thank you.

And thanks to every single reader who has left a review, signed up to my mailing list, spoken to me on Facebook or emailed me. You make my dreams a reality. I'm overwhelmed by the support and can't wait to share more with you!

And a final shout out to Louise again. Thank you for being there for me when I felt nobody else was and for helping me through the deep water I found myself in earlier this year. Your friendship and support, both professional and personal, means the world to me. I think I'd be lost without you.

About The Author

Lisa is an author of new adult romance and writes both paranormal and contemporary.

In between running a business, looking after her family and writing, Lisa sometimes finds spare time to do other things. This often involves swapping her book worlds for gaming worlds. She even leaves the house occasionally.

Lisa is originally from the UK but moved to Australia in 2001 and now lives in Perth in Western Australia with her husband, three children and dog.

For more information about her new releases subscribe to her newsletter:
http://eepurl.com/Po81D

Facebook
www.facebook.com/lisaswallowbooks

Website
www.lisaswallow.net

A full list of Lisa's available books can be found at:
www.amazon.com/author/lisaswallow

She can be contacted by email at:
lisa@lisaswallow.net

Lisa Swallow

CPSIA information can be obtained
at www.ICGtesting.com
Printed in the USA
LVOW12s1458041016
507373LV00001B/75/P